In Her Image

by
Satinmaid

Copyright 2016 Satinmaid
This ebook is licensed for your personal enjoyment only.
This ebook may not be re-sold or given away to other people.
Thank you for respecting the hard work of this author.

One

I first met Joanna and Julie at a nightclub. They were by far the most interesting thing to look at: a pair of gorgeous red headed identical twin sisters. They were tall in their high heels, their flaming locks fell in glorious curls past their shoulders and they were wearing matching figure hugging velvet dresses one in black and the other in dark green. The dresses had low-cut scoop necklines with long sleeves and short, flared skirts that came almost to mid-thigh. Each wore a pair of black suede high heeled knee boots that laced all the way up the back. Both wore scarlet lipstick with dark eye liner, large hoop earrings and a tiny silver necklace with the letter 'J' hanging from it.

Instantly I found myself wanting to get to know them better. As they danced on the floor I watched and noticed that they appeared to be looking for something. Several men asked one or other - or both - of them to dance but were immediately turned down with annoyed frowns. They got the same sort of response at the bar. They didn't have to pay for drinks but didn't want the men buying to hang around and annoy them. There were a good few disappointed men there.

After watching a dozen or do men get shot down in flames by this gorgeous pair I gave up any thought of getting to know them. I was surprised when ten minutes later they sat down on either side of me and the one in the green dress asked if they could buy me a drink. I was too shocked to answer so I just nodded, drinking in the sight of her perfect face with its beautiful beaming smile. The one in the black dress was studying me in silence and suddenly looked satisfied, as if a decision had been reached.

They introduced themselves. The one in the black dress was Joanna and her sister in the green dress was Julie. We spent the evening chatting, dancing and drinking. I felt on a natural high knowing how many men in that club saw me dancing with both of these lovely sisters and were jealous. Plenty of men tried to cut in and dance with one of them but they were having none of it and clung tightly to me, pressing their bodies close as they danced. The evening passed in a whirl and I found myself sitting with Julie on my lap kissing me full on the mouth, my hand up her skirt caressing her gorgeous thighs while Joanna caressed my neck and asked if I wanted to come home with them. I stopped kissing Julie and said I would love to. Julie slipped off my lap and said she was going to powder her nose. Joanna leant over and carried on kissing where Julie had left off.

A while later we were pulling up in the cab outside their house. Their town house apparently. They claimed that they also owned a large house in the country somewhere. Judging by the size of the town house and the area they lived in I was quite prepared to believe it. As I paid the cabbie he was craning his neck to see the two women and winked at me as Julie dragged me towards the house.

Inside Joanna led me upstairs to a large bedroom with a huge bed. There would be room enough and plenty to spare in that bed for all three of us. Joanna started to kiss me again and Julie reappeared with a bottle of champagne and three glasses. Joanna lounged on the bed while Julie poured the champagne and handed us both a glass. She sipped from her glass then put her arm round my neck and pulled me close for a long kiss.

Joanna got up from the bed and Julie sat at a large dressing table. She began to brush her hair, half watching what she was doing and half watching Joanna and me in the mirror. Joanna began to kiss me now.

We kissed for a minute before Joanna pulled my top off over my head. I reached to unzip her dress but she pushed my hands away. I settled for gripping her bottom and pulling her towards me. She caressed my chest with her hands and I heard both girls moan with pleasure. I looked over Joanna's shoulder as she kissed me and saw Julie removing her dress to reveal silk panties, bra and suspender belt that were the same dark green as her dress. I could see that her dress must have only just covered the lacy tops of her stockings. She was still wearing the knee-boots and looked even more amazing than she had in the dress.

Joanna pulled away from me and for a second I thought she might be annoyed that I had been looking at her sister. She wasn't annoyed, she just stepped back and Julie stepped forward and began kissing me and touching my chest. I enjoyed the change and flowed with her kiss as I ran my hands over her silk clad bottom and she began to undo the button fly of my jeans. After she had undone the top one she pulled the rest open with a flick of her hand. She let the jeans fall round my ankles then stepped away again.

Joanna walked towards me and knelt down. She had removed her dress, boots and bra and was kneeling before me in just her stockings, suspenders and panties. These matched the ones worn by Julie but were black instead of green. These girls obviously believed in having a colour scheme for their clothes. She kissed my erection through my underpants and her hard nipples brushed my thighs. I ran my fingers through her wonderful fiery hair as she untied my shoelaces and removed my shoes, socks and trousers. She kissed both my feet, her hair gently brushing them as she did so, and stood up to let Julie take over.

Julie had now removed all except her green silk panties. They were the style that tied up with a ribbon at each side. A couple of tugs and they would be easily removed and that thought turned me on even more so I was completely hard when Julie slipped me from my underpants and let them drop to the floor as she stared at my erection with a hungry look on her face. She kissed it as she removed my underpants from round my ankles and I now ran my hands through her hair.

She stood up and lifted her hand to my lips. "Open wide," she said. I glanced down to see a small pink pill between her fingers.

"What is it?" I asked. I'd never taken drugs before and was a little nervous about it.

"Just something to make you feel good," she purred. She pressed the pill between my lips and in my thoroughly aroused state I let her pop it into my mouth. She gave me a sip from her glass and I swallowed it before I had a chance to worry too much about what it was.

Julie stepped back with a smile on her face.

"Aren't you going to have a pill too?"

"No," she grinned, "just you."

I could see Joanna standing in just her panties and, as Julie stepped back to let me see her better, Joanna slowly – oh! so slowly - pulled the ribbon on each side of her panties as she stared me right in the eye. Julie moved away and turned to watch. She kept looking first at my erection then at Joanna pulling the ribbons of her panties. Suddenly the knots holding Joanna's panties came undone and she let them fall to the floor. She was obviously a natural redhead.

She stepped forward and began kissing me again, backing me onto the bed. I sat down then turned round and lay back on the huge bed as Joanna pushed me. I moved to the centre of the bed and Joanna made me lay my arms out away from my side with my palms up. She climbed on the bed one side of me and Julie moved round and climbed on the other side. Each of them grabbed a wrist and put it between their legs as they knelt next to me. I pushed my finger into Joanna and she gasped and wiggled, her grip on my wrist becoming tighter. I could feel Julie through the silk of her panties and wanted to push inside her as well. She was gripping my wrist too tight for me to get hold of the ribbons holding her panties on.

I was used like this until both the women came to orgasm, nearly simultaneously. It was amazing, I didn't know which one to look at; both looked incredible in the throes of pleasure. Whatever was in the pill seemed to be having an effect on me. I was feeling light-headed and very sensual and my vision softened, making everything in the room look like it was through soft focus lens.

My hands were still trapped between their thighs and their touches on my body were sending waves of pleasure through me like nothing I'd ever experienced before.

I felt that I would only need a slight touch to explode into orgasm myself. The sisters started kissing me. They leant forwards and made me kiss, nibble, lick and suck each of their nipples in turn. The drug was making everything feel amazing and I was fascinated by the feel of their hard nipples against my tongue. They kept my hands clamped between their thighs and used a hand each taking it in turns to gently stroke my erection. I wanted to be able to move and touch them but I was helpless, each caress making me moan and writhe beneath them, unable to think straight or do anything except lie there in a rapturous trance as they used me.

When they sensed that I was about to come they removed their hands from my erection and went back to kissing me for a while. Then Joanna straddled her legs across my chest, pinning my shoulders and leant forward for me to kiss her breasts. They weren't large but they were absolutely beautiful, the loveliest I had ever seen. I could feel Julie kissing my inner thigh, her hair brushing the other one and nearly driving me crazy. Although my shoulders were pinned, my hands were now mostly free and I managed to caress Joanna's bottom as she straddled me.

Joanna shuffled forward until her crotch was in reach of my mouth. I began to kiss her and she moaned softly, writhing at the touch of my lips and tongue between her legs. Meanwhile Julie was kissing my erection then straddled me also, brushing against me with her silk panties. I couldn't see her do it but I felt her panties slide against my erection as she untied them and removed them. The feeling of the silk against me made me cry out in wonder. She wiggled slightly, teasing the tip of my cock then allowed me to slide into her. The two women straddling me had pinned my arms with their legs and I lay helpless on the bed as one of them made me use my mouth on her and the other made me penetrate her. I had never felt so helpless or so turned on as I did then. Every time I came near climax Julie stopped moving and only finally allowed me to orgasm as Joanna succumbed to my tongue and shuddered in ecstasy. When I came it was like my entire body was on fire and there were starbursts behind my eyes.

They kissed and stroked me until I fell asleep, one of them lying in each arm. It was an imprisonment I was happy to accept for the night.

I woke the next morning to find my wrists and ankles tied to the bed with silk scarves and the girls taking it in turns to kiss and suck my erection. I was just about to come when they stopped. Julie looked me straight in the eyes and very gently kissed the tip of my cock with her scarlet painted lips. The lipstick left a mark and combined with the kiss was just enough to finish me off. They sat back looking excited as they watched me orgasm and spurt over myself and the bedclothes between my legs. I suddenly felt extremely vulnerable and humiliated and struggled to move but my wrists and ankles were tied tight. They watched until my climax was over then mopped me up with tissues, sensuously and very gently, before they untied me.

I saw them again a couple of nights later, then again two nights after that. Soon I was spending whole weekends at their town house and every time I saw them they double teamed me like that, each time making me take one of those small pink pills that made me feel like I was in paradise and left me helpless at the slightest touch from one of them and seemed to sap my will and remove any urge I had to object to anything they wanted to do to me. Under the influence of whatever they were giving me, I was helpless to resist whenever they tied me to the bed, teasing me for what felt like hours and making me beg for the merest chance to touch them.

After a couple of months I was completely under their spell. I was head over heels in love with them both and even when I was away from them and not under the influence of those little pink pills I couldn't stop thinking about them. I was a man obsessed. They were on my mind constantly. I couldn't concentrate on anything and my work suffered. There was no comedown from the pills but if I spent an evening alone, being apart from them felt worse than any horror stories I'd heard about drug withdrawal. I neglected my friends, wanting only to spend time with the sisters. Even when I knew that I wasn't going to be seeing them I refused any offers to socialise in case they changed their minds and called. I sat in my bedroom trying not to cry and feeling distraught, literally panicking that I would never hear from them again. When they did call me to meet up I was pathetically grateful and was entirely at their beck and call, never once refusing to come when I was summoned and never once plucking up the resolve to question why I had become like this or what they were doing to me. I was a wreck unless I was with Joanna and Julie and after a while my friends stopped even trying to get me to go out with them and I didn't really notice or care as long as I was going to see the sisters.

Two

The time came when I finished a job I was doing and had nothing else lined up – not that anybody would want to hire me any more as my work had deteriorated so badly in my obsession with Joanna and Julie. The sisters invited me to their country house for a fortnight. I accepted like a shot; by that point I would have crawled over broken glass to spend just five minutes kissing their feet. The house was in the middle of the West Country miles from anywhere. The nearest village was five miles away and the nearest main road was three miles away. The land was beautiful, forested all the way round. You could almost imagine that the rest of the world didn't exist and that only these lands were real. It was a place to get away from it all, nothing would disturb you here. I had realised that they had lots of money but I hadn't realised that they were this rich.

Julie had given me a pink pill when they arrived at my house and I was in a trance most of the way there with Joanna stroking my thigh as Julie drove the Jag. I eventually nodded off and only woke as we pulled up the gravel driveway to their country home, so I wasn't at all sure where we were. They hadn't mentioned where the house was and it had never occurred to me to ask.

For the first day all I saw of the house was the marble floored hall, the gorgeous oak staircase, the bathroom with the huge tub and antique brass fittings and the bedroom.

Mostly the bedroom.

Joanna and Julie mostly kept me tied to the bed when they weren't using me. I know it seems a bit weird but it was by no means unpleasant and I had no will left. Each pink pill just drew me further and further under their control.

The bed was a huge four poster, even bigger than the bed in the town house. I was given another pill and led straight up there when we arrived and after our lovemaking held them both in my arms while we napped. I again woke to find myself bound to the bed and being kissed by the sisters. This time they didn't untie me when they had finished. Julie plumped my pillows up and untied my ankles so I could sit up. I was kept like this for the whole day, only being untied to go to the bathroom. I was too far gone to resist or object; if these two beautiful sexy women wanted me tied to the bed while they pampered me and made love to me then I would let them and gladly. The two of them took turns feeding me then went back to teasing and stroking me for a while. They teased me until I begged them to release me, then teased me some more. When I started crying and pleading with them not to tease me any more they finally relented and took turns kissing my cock until I came. I fell asleep still tied to the bed, with Joanna and Julie each gently sucking and licking a nipple.

I again awoke to find myself bound and being used. Another bout of lovemaking ensued before Julie left the room and Joanna carried on touching me very gently with the tips of her fingernails. Somewhere deep inside, through the haze of my obsession with them, I knew that the idea of keeping me tied up was strange and I was wondering if they were going to keep me like this for the entire fortnight. I begged Joanna to untie me and let me touch and kiss her. I wanted to so badly as I had been tied up and unable to touch them for a whole day. She just smiled and carried on teasing my erection.

Finally she untied me and led me through to the bathroom. Julie had filled the bath with steaming water and flowery smelling bath salts. I was naked so I stepped straight into the tub. Joanna was naked as well and sat down behind me. I could feel her nipples against my back and she reached round to feel between my legs. Julie was wearing just her panties and leaned over the bathtub to kiss me. Joanna started to soap my back and Julie soaped my chest. After that the two of them washed my hair, Joanna in the bath with me and Julie leaning over. Julie left us alone again and Joanna started to soap between my legs.

When I had gone hard she whispered in my ear, "I think we'd better get you back in the bedroom so you can use that."

We climbed out and she handed me a fluffy pink bathrobe to put on. We dried ourselves then she took my bathrobe from me and led me naked and obedient into the bedroom. Julie had cleared the dinner things away and had put on a long, dark green satin nightdress. It clung to every curve of her body and swished about her ankles. One of the shoestring straps had slipped down over her shoulder, exposing the top of her left breast. I gasped as she stepped forwards to kiss me roughly and passionately. When I surfaced Joanna had changed into a matching black nightgown and was holding a pink nightie in her hands.

"Do you like these nighties?" she asked. I nodded in mute appreciation of their forms in the sexy, clinging satin.

"How much do you like them?" asked Julie with an enigmatic smile.

"After you two they are the most wonderful things I have ever seen." I replied in a daze.

"Really?" asked Joanna and I nodded again. "Glad you like them, we love them as well. Do you like pink?"

I ached to please her so I told her it was my favourite colour. I didn't get any further as Julie started to kiss me again, her satin clad body sliding provocatively against mine. Joanna started to kiss the back of my neck and the feeling of these two both moving against me in their nighties was incredible. Joanna took hold of my wrists and lifted my arms above my head. I didn't pay much attention to what she was doing as Julie was a very good kisser. Suddenly I felt cool satin sliding down over my arms and head. Both of them stepped back slightly and tugged the long pink nightie down over my body. Except for the colour it was exactly the same as the ones they were wearing.

I didn't get any time to question it as Julie kissed me roughly, forcing her tongue into my mouth and driving all thoughts from my head. Joanna was kissing the back of my neck again and the feeling of our three bodies rubbing together, each wearing the sexy material made me forget about protesting. I was led to the bed and laid down in my nightie. Julie smoothed the nightie down over my body. It reached all the way to my ankles. They began kissing me all over through the satin. I was too turned on to resist even slightly when they grabbed a wrist each and tied them to the bed with pink silk scarves.

Julie carried on kissing me through the nightie, making me moan and writhe while Joanna tied my ankles to the bed. Through the haze that passed for my thought processes these days I wondered what new thing they had in mind as so far they had only tied me to the bed after we had had sex, not before. Obviously they had planned for me to be tightly bound in a pink satin nightdress when I found out what they had in mind.

Once I was tightly tied, ankles and wrists, in my nightie, they each gave me a lingering kiss on the lips. They shared a glance and, at a quick nod from Joanna, Julie ran from the bedroom.

"What's going on?" I asked, confused. Joanna just shushed me.

A few moments later, Julie and came back with several hypodermic needles and two vials of liquid on a tray.

"What's going on?" I asked again, actually starting to get nervous – the nearest thing I'd had to a thought for myself in several weeks. Were they going to give me a different drug from the pink pills? What would that do to me?

I struggled but was held tight by the silk scarves as Julie prepared two syringes while Joanna climbed onto the bed.

I mumbled feebly, "What are you doing? Don't…" but Joanna put her finger to my lips and whispered, "Don't struggle darling, we won't hurt you."

There was nothing I could do to stop them as Julie handed Joanna a syringe and she pulled down the front of my nightie and injected me twice in the chest, an inch or two beneath each nipple. I was too confused to be able to work out what was happening. Julie prepared another syringe and Joanna injected me again, in the arm this time.

"What is it? Heroin?"

"Shhh," replied Joanna. "You'll like what they do to you and you'll love what *we* do to you when they begin to have an effect." She kissed me, stopping any more protests and I relaxed a little and felt a stirring between my legs. The injections had been made now and there was nothing I could do about it. I wasn't keen but surely they wouldn't do anything dangerous? Julie popped another pink pill into my mouth and carefully let me sip from a bottle of water to swallow it.

With nothing else I could do I laid back and let them use me in the nightie. I began to feel lightheaded as the pill began to work. I was also starting to feel all warm and tingly, happy and comfortable. They took great pleasure in touching me through the pink satin and telling me how pretty I looked in it. They were obviously extremely turned on and I couldn't help responding and feeling oddly pretty under their intense, loving gazes. They touched and kissed me through the satin, never quite touching my erection, which drove me wild with desire and frustration. They made me kiss their breasts through their nighties and slipped their straps from their shoulders for me to suck their hard nipples.

A look passed between them and they knelt each side of me and bent down to kiss my erection through the nightie. My eyes rolled back in my head at this sensation and I moaned softly on the bed, completely back under their spell.

Their hands caressed my belly and thighs through the satin. They stopped kissing me and moved their hands so that they were both holding my stiff manhood. They both looked and saw how lovingly I was gazing at them then stared deep into each other's eyes.

They began to kiss. Julie moaned slightly as Joanna forced her tongue into Julie's mouth. Their grips on my erection tightened and they began to rub me through the satin. I was shocked to see the sisters kissing each other. They looked up and smiled.

"Surprised darling?" asked Joanna, "We're not really sisters you know. We're not related at all. Show him Julie." I looked and Julie said, "Yes mistress," and began to lift the hem of her nightie up. I saw that she was apparently not a redhead but a blonde. I suddenly realised that I hadn't seen her without panties on before. Every time she had made love to me I was either tied down and couldn't see her or Joanna was straddling my chest making me use my tongue on her which also meant that I couldn't see Julie and of course, all of those times I was under the influence of those pink pills and completely unable to think coherently or notice such a fact.

"I met Julie at university," said Joanna. "People said that we looked a bit alike. We look a lot more alike now after her figure training and dyeing her hair. I got to know her and fell in love with her and I knew I could make her even more perfect."

They were still caressing me through the satin, making it virtually impossible to take in what Joanna was saying. "I don't understand," I mumbled.

"I remade her in my image. I seduced and dominated her. I changed her appearance and made her my double." They were still rubbing me through the nightie and I really wasn't taking this all in. I couldn't help but enjoy the feeling of their touches and was too desperate for them to continue what they were doing to me to worry about what she was saying. They each slipped a hand up under the nightie and I gasped at this new, wonderful sensation of them forcing their hands up the satin skirt of the nightdress that I wore. I felt vulnerable but I loved it.

"I've always preferred women to men," continued Joanna as they fondled me, "but Julie, or Kelly as she was called when I met her, likes both. She has talked about the two of us bedding a man and turning him into one of us, making him over in my image too. After a while I came to like the idea as well - although I wasn't so sure about letting the man stay a man."

"What man?" I muttered, thoroughly confused as to why they were talking about some man when they had me there.

Julie giggled, "You, silly. We're going to make you into Joanna's double too."

Was she seriously saying that they were going to try to turn me into one of them as Joanna had transformed Julie - or Kelly or whatever she was really called - into her sister? I couldn't tell if she really meant it. I was so addled that I half believed I was imagining it and completely misunderstanding something.

Joanna continued, "The female hormones and the anti-androgen we gave you will make you grow breasts and act in a more feminine way. The pink pills have been making you more compliant and very suggestible. We're going to train you to act as a woman and make you look like us. You are going to be so beautiful. You will be ours forever."

There was such a look of love in both their eyes and they were still rubbing me. I couldn't help responding although a nagging voice far down inside me was telling me that I should be worrying about something. They only just lifted the hem of the nightie in time for my orgasm. I spurted all over my legs and their hands. They wiped it up with tissues and pulled the hem of the nightie back down to my ankles. Joanna carried on talking to me while Julie searched for more silk scarves in the dressing table.

"I'm going to make you submissive and feminine," continued Joanna. "I'll train you to be a woman and you can be with us for the rest of your life. Obviously I'll have to punish you if you disobey me but you might even learn to like me spanking you – Julie certainly learned to enjoy it."

My confused mind grasped this bit of information. "I don't want to be spanked," I frowned. "I'll be good." I felt like crying at the thought of Joanna being angry with me.

"I like spanking. It's all for your own good. One day you will be a beautiful woman and have both of us every night forever."

She touched me gently through the nightie as she spoke. Her touches were starting to arouse me again but it was too soon to get another erection.

"We really love you and we just want to make you more perfect." She smiled at Julie. "Julie wants to keep your little cock but as I already said, I prefer women. If you fail to please us with it then I might decide to see if you are more pleasing without it. I know a special clinic and I have enough money and enough dirt on certain people – including a very good surgeon - to get it removed without your permission and with no questions asked and no chance of any comeback. I did my research before I agreed to Julie's plan so don't make the mistake of thinking that I don't know exactly what I am doing. You are going to be a woman, even if you keep your little cock, and there's nothing you can do about it. Make the best of it."

She looked round to check that Julie was still by the dressing table then whispered to me, "You might decide that you want to get rid of it anyway, to please me. I'll arrange a full sex-change operation if you beg nicely. But whether you get turned into a real woman or just have it chopped off, I'd love to get rid of it so we can all wear really tight sexy skirts together without any horrible bulges ruining the front of your skirt."

There was an excited look in her eye and a happy smile on her face as she continued aloud, "I did promise Julie that I would probably let you keep your cock to please her but give me an excuse to have it cut off as a punishment and I think I would just orgasm on the spot!" She really did look thrilled at the thought. "I still haven't decided that I will definitely let you keep it and I'll be more than happy to get it chopped off if you displease me. The only reason it's staying there for the moment is that Julie blubbed and begged me not to. So you'd better hope she never changes her mind. The minute she's bored with your little willy – off it comes."

Whatever the pink pills were, they had done their job over the last few months and stopped me getting scared. I giggled – it was funny hearing it called my 'little willy'. Without the effects of those pink pills over the last couple of months I surely would have been screaming and struggling at the thought of having my cock cut off. Instead, the only concept that managed to push through the fog of my consciousness was that Joanna wanted me to make her happy. I smiled happily, sure that Joanna was just teasing about all the confusing things she had just threatened me with and wouldn't really do that to me, especially as I loved them both and wanted to please them too.

Julie walked back over to the bed and Joanna said, "We'll untie you from the bed now and start your transformation and training. From this moment on you will refer to us as 'Mistress Joanna' and 'Miss Julie'. Is that understood Jenny?"

I didn't answer and she smiled and said to me, "Your new name is Jenny, darling. Do you like it?"

Her smile was so wonderful that I just nodded, anything they called me sounded good to me just then as the pink pill began to take full effect. She smiled again and repeated what she had said before.

"You will call us 'Mistress Joanna' and 'Miss Julie'. Is that understood Jenny?"

The drugs were making me feel very good inside so I smiled and said, "Yes darling. I love you both and I want to please you."

She smiled and kissed me. "We love you very much too, but I told you to refer to me as 'Mistress Joanna'. You'll learn in time otherwise I'm afraid that I'll have to spank you until you learn to be a good girl."

"I'll be good Mistress Joanna, I won't forget again. You don't have to spank me." I started to cry, distressed at the thought of displeasing her. "Please don't punish me. It's the pink pill you gave me, I'm not thinking too clearly. It's nice though and I do love you. I just wish you didn't have to spank me."

"Oh, but we must. You'll never learn otherwise. Julie had to be spanked until she cried almost every day for a month. I didn't know about these pills then and had to put a lot of effort into training her. I had to humiliate her in dozens of different ways before she finally realised that she was helpless and completely at my mercy. She's glad I did though, aren't you Julie?" Joanna was caressing my nipple through the satin nightie and touching Julie between her legs through her nightie as she spoke.

Julie curtseyed and said, "Yes mistress. You made me more perfect and I'll love you forever for doing it. I'm sure Jenny will love you forever when you turn her into one of us."

"See?" said Joanne, turning back to me. "It's all for you really. You'll thank me for it too when you see how beautiful we make you. Things won't be as difficult for you as they were for Julie. The pills are working wonderfully and you've become far more dependent on me a lot faster than Julie did. But that doesn't mean you won't get spanked. We *want* to spank you. You can't stop us and you might even enjoy it. You won't believe how happy I will make you if you just surrender to my commands and submit to me totally. And you won't believe the things I will do to you if you displease me."

"We'll untie you from the bed now. Do everything we say or you will be punished." She leant close and whispered again, as her fingers gently stroked my still-soft penis through the satin nightie, "And you know what punishment you'll get if you really misbehave. If you're a very bad girl then I might decide you don't need your little willy."

She kissed me and untied my ankles from the bed. Then she untied my wrists and allowed me to sit up. "Stand up Jenny and face me."

I did so and turned to face her as she sat on the bed.

"Oh, did I forget to mention? Whenever one of us gives you an order you must say 'Yes Mistress Joanna' or 'Yes Miss Julie' and curtsey if you are standing. We'll show you how to curtsey properly later. Let's see how well you do at it now. Go on."

"Yes Mistress Joanna," I said and tried to curtsey, gripping the skirt of the nightie and not doing it very well because I felt light headed and had never even tried before.

"Not too bad but you need some practice. That's for later. Now let Julie take your wrists."

Julie reached out and grabbed my wrists, pulling them behind me. She began to tie them together with a silk scarf. Joanna frowned.

"Did you forget to say something Jenny?"

"Sorry Mistress Joanna. I apologise, I'm still getting used to this. I meant to say 'yes Mistress' when you gave me that order. Please don't punish me for it."

"Don't try to get out of it. If you carry on doing that then I may force you to beg me for punishment and the longer you resist begging for it, the worse your punishment will be. Understood?"

"Yes Mistress Joanna." I couldn't curtsey with my hands tied behind my back. Fortunately she didn't seem to mind the lapse.

They both fondled and kissed me as I stood there in my pink satin nightie. Julie said to me, "Be a good girl and we'll make you feel so wonderful you won't believe it. Up until now we've been turned on by just the idea of making you a girl like us; imagine how good we'll be to you when you actually *are* a girl."

I was still woolly headed and rather than being scared of becoming a girl I found myself getting turned on imagining how passionate they would be when I was. It would quite possibly be worth it. Surely it would just be for a while, whenever we came to this country house. They weren't talking about keeping me as a girl forever were they? I believed Joanna when she said that she knew exactly what she was doing, even if I didn't quite understand all the things she was saying about keeping my willy. Where would it go? I knew that I had missed something and couldn't quite work out what. Anyway, there was nothing I could do about it. I was bewitched by these two women. I knew I couldn't stop them and had no will left to even want to stop them. I was sure that anything they wanted to do to me that made them happy would also make me happy.

It was in no state to realise how serious they were about it all. I was drugged and in love and really didn't believe that they were going to do it or really understand what they were saying to me. I thought it was just another bizarre sexual fantasy to act out.

They led me into a room I hadn't seen yet. It was next to the bedroom but the door had always been closed when I had gone past it to the bathroom. At those times I was escorted anyway and was too busy enjoying the sensation of being pampered and touched by these two and too lacking in any critical facilities to bother asking what was in there. It turned out to be a huge exercise room with various a large matted area in the middle, plenty of gym equipment and an assortment of cupboards round the walls.

"First we'll give you a massage," said Joanna. "Your figure isn't right and massage will help break up your fat deposits and make the figure training work better. We bought you some lovely corsets and basques. Regular massage will help them shape you more efficiently and you'll have to wear them for less time before your body is right and you can wear sexy bras and panties to match ours. In pink of course. That's your colour. I wear black, Julie wears green and now you wear pink. You did say it was your favourite colour didn't you Jenny?"

I struggled to remember if I had. I remembered the pink nightie they'd put on me and had a vague memory of being asked about the colour. I hadn't been thinking when I said that pink was my favourite colour but I didn't want to disappoint Joanna and didn't want her to feel bad about having to spank me if I lied. In fact, the more I thought about it, the more it seemed like I must have said that, if Joanna thought that I had.

"Yes Mistress Joanna. It's one of my favourites anyway. I would never have worn it though."

"Are you saying that you don't want to wear pink Jenny? It was Julie's idea to make you wear pink as you are a man that we are making girly. She thought that it would be more fitting that you wear the girliest colour. Julie thought you might even come to like the idea of always wearing pink. I hope she isn't…upset…with you if you don't like her idea." She stroked the small bulge of my cock under the nightie as she said this. "I know you're having trouble thinking straight at the moment but you really do need to get this idea into your head. If you displease me, I will cut your willy off. Understand?"

I frowned, why was she saying that again? You can't just cut someone's willy off, can you? They don't grow back. Or do they? I couldn't remember for sure. It was too difficult to think about and I grasped at the reason she was talking about that again, as that seemed a lot easier to understand than what was being said to me. "I meant that I like pink but would never have thought of wearing it myself. I'm glad that Mistress Julie wants me to wear pink. Now I've worn this pink nightie I think the colour suits me. Thank you for choosing pink to be my colour."

"Good, I'm glad you agree with the choice. Untie him Julie."

Julie curtseyed and said, "Yes mistress." She untied my wrists and I was ordered to remove the nightie and lie down on a massage table in the room. I attempted another curtsey, glad of an instruction to follow so I didn't have to try to understand everything that was happening and being said to me. "Yes Mistress Joanna." Julie took my wrists again and tied them to metal bars sticking out from the top of the table. Next she took my ankles and tied each to a stirrup at the end of the table so that my legs were held open. There followed more than an hour of pummelling, pressing, kneading and fondling before they untied me. Joanna and Julie stopped frequently to kiss and grope each other and I was untied once so that I could be turned face down before my wrists and ankles were again secured and the massage continued on my back. Finally I was allowed to stand and was led to the bathroom with my wrists tied in front of me.

The bathroom was huge, almost a suite of rooms by itself. It had a large freestanding bath at one side with a sink and large lit mirror next to it. Separated by a glass door, there was a large walk-in shower that was almost as big as the bedroom at my flat. They made me stand naked in the bathroom covered in a sharp smelling cream while Julie painted my fingernails a bright pink colour, telling me that I would be growing my own fingernails and learning how to paint them myself. Then she untied me and led me into the shower. As I stood under the water, the cream washed off, taking all my sparse blonde body hair with it. They had spared only my eyebrows and lashes, head hair and pubic hair. Correction, most of my pubic hair. Joanna had applied it carefully and what washed away left hair in the shape of a heart framing my manhood.

My hands were tied in front of me and I was ordered to sit on a stool and tip my head back and Julie began to apply something to my hair, which was almost shoulder length as they had persuaded me over the months I knew them to let it grow longer. Joanna applied something to my pubic region, flicking my cock into submission when I started to get an erection from her touch. I was left tied up while they applied scented body lotion. Their hands felt amazing, sliding over my newly smooth body. My toenails were varnished to match my fingernails and when they had dried I was untied and sent back into the shower to rinse what was left of my hair.

I looked down while showering and realised that Joanna had dyed my pubic hair. It was now a bright pink heart. When I got out of the shower and looked at my hair I saw that it had been dyed a fiery red like the two women's. I didn't get much time to process any of this because I was taken back into the exercise room for some more massage before they forced me into my first corset. It was pink, obviously, and was laced tighter than I would have imagined them to be but it wasn't too bad and only took me a short while to get used to it. The corset was made of satin at the front and some tight, slightly stretchy material at the sides and back. The cups were not boned but were very tight under my arms and pushed what little flesh I did have into their shape. I was bemused to see that I had tiny breasts!

Joanna saw me staring at them and said, "Don't worry Jenny, they'll get bigger when the hormones take effect. Soon they will be as big as mine and Julie's. I can't wait until you're a 'C' cup as well! You really want to have real women's breasts don't you Jenny?"

"But....but....." I stammered. Did I? That didn't seem right, did it? I didn't know for sure.

"That wasn't a question Jenny. It was an order. You want to have breasts don't you?" She smiled sweetly and glanced significantly at my pink-heart framed cock. Still not certain, I curtseyed and said, "Yes Mistress Joanna."

"Yes what, darling?"

"I want to have breasts."

She frowned, "You mean, 'I want to have breasts *please*, Mistress Joanna,' don't you? If you want to keep your cock, I mean."

"Sorry Mistress," I curtseyed. She seemed sure of what she was saying so I supposed that I must have got it wrong. I did want to keep my cock after all. "I do want to have breasts, please Mistress Joanna. Will they be as pretty as yours?" I hoped that if I was nicer she might be happier with me and forgive my misunderstanding. I still wasn't really sure what was happening to me but I thought that as long as I tried my best to make her happy then everything would work out okay. Oddly though, as I said it, I did sort of want my breasts to be as nice as hers. I'd never seen more perfect breasts so why wouldn't I want mine to be as pretty?

She smiled, "Of course they will, they'll be the same size as mine. That's the whole point of this."

I smiled in response, happy that despite my confusion I had apparently worked out the correct answer to her question. "Thank you, Mistress Joanna."

Feeling a little relieved that I hadn't upset her, I allowed them to continue dressing me. Sheer black silk stockings were drawn up my legs and attached to the suspenders on the corset. This was another totally new sensation for me. The combination of the pills, my smooth legs, the lush feel of the stockings and the caressing touches as they were put on me made me moan with pleasure. I moaned again and was getting very hard when they put tight pink satin panties on me.

As Joanna stood up from this last task I tried to kiss her. She frowned and pulled away.

"I don't remember giving you permission to do that Jenny! Do I need to give you a spanking?"

"It would be worth it," I sighed, "to kiss you." I tried again and this time Julie leapt on me from behind and roughly pulled my arms back, dragging me away from Joanna and tying my wrists behind me.

"That's it Jenny. You're getting punished now. Immediately." Joanna sat on the edge of the bath and Julie dragged me over to her, forcing me to bend forward over Joanna's lap. Joanna gripped my wrists and held me firmly over her knees. She was touching me lightly through the panties as she said, "You tried to kiss me twice without being ordered to do so and failed to call me Mistress. Now you must be made to understand that I am serious about all this. I will not have such disobedience from you and it seems you need a little taster of what your punishment will be to make you behave."

I began to wriggle furiously, not wanting to be punished and worrying that I might be wrong about this arrangement only lasting for the fortnight. There was a loud slap and a sudden stinging sensation in my rear as Joanna raised her arm and brought her hand sharply down on my bottom. Stunned, I froze for a second then began to wriggle, if anything even more desperately than before. Julie was clapping her hands, jumping up and down and giggling with delight. There was another slap and Joanna said, "Stay still and accept your punishment, you'll only make it worse for yourself if you struggle and be disobedient."

"Yes Mistress Joanna," I mumbled, finally starting to believe that maybe she was serious.

"Julie, go through into the bedroom while I punish Jenny."

Julie pouted, "I wanted to see him being spanked."

"You will have plenty of chances to see him being spanked. I hope I won't have to be punishing you as well?"

"No Mistress, I'll be a good girl as always."

Joanna smiled, "See Jenny? It's not difficult to be a good girl; just do everything I say. You don't have to make any choices for yourself any more. Just completely submit to me. Run along now Julie, get the bedroom ready for when I bring our naughty little girl back in. She should be a bit better behaved by then."

"Yes Mistress," curtseyed Julie and went towards the door. I looked pleadingly at Julie, hoping she would do something to help me and not wanting her to leave - not when Joanna kept talking about cutting my willy off and I was just about able to grasp the fact that Julie was the only thing stopping that from happening. She just grinned, stuck her tongue out at me and left, closing the door behind her. Mistress Joanna went back to caressing me through the panties and although I was a little worried, I was rapidly forgetting what it was I had been worried about. Her touches felt good and I'm sure she could feel me go hard against her thighs through the satin I was wearing.

"Now Jenny, tell me why you're being punished."

I struggled to remember. "I was naughty Mistress Joanna. I think I tried to kiss you without permission?"

"Sort of. You're being punished because I don't think you're taking this seriously enough. You have already done several things to earn punishment and I think you might have carried on being naughty. I want to make you realise that you are mine now. I can do anything I want to you. Anything." Her hand slipped between my legs and her fingernails cupped my balls, digging in slightly. Not enough to hurt, just enough to get across the point that she had me at her mercy.

"Maybe you don't think I mean everything I say, or that I can't do it. If that's the case, you're very wrong and if you don't learn to behave very soon then you will be getting a demonstration of just how serious I am. A very permanent demonstration that even you won't be able to misunderstand." Her hand slipped further, touching my erection through the panties. "I promised Julie that I would let her keep your cock, at least for now. I made no such promises about your balls." Her hand paused, "Or maybe you like being punished and that's why you're naughty? Maybe you *want* me to send you to the clinic to have your cock chopped off." Her voice was excited, clearly aroused by the thought, "If you want me to force you into it then I would be pleased to do so."

My erection shrivelled as she spoke. It wasn't sounding funny any more and I was pretty sure that I *didn't* want my cock cut off.

"Do you want to go to the clinic Jenny?"

"No Mistress, please don't make me. I'll be good. I promise."

Joanna laughed, "Then I guess I *am* punishing you for not taking me seriously enough. Well, here's what punishment you get for general disobedience. You already know what's in store for you if you seriously misbehave." Without warning she slapped me hard on the bottom. I yelped in surprise and pain as well as humiliation and distress that I had upset her. "Just a dozen or so for you now Jenny. Do you think that will be enough to make you behave for a while?"

"Yes Mistress. Ow!" She had slapped me again as I answered her. The rest of the spanks followed while she told me how naughty I was and how disappointed she was in me. By the fourth I was begging her to stop, promising to be good just to end the spanking. By the sixth I was biting my lip and determined to behave for my Mistress. By the tenth I was pleading incoherently with her, begging her to believe me when I promised to be good for her. By the last – and I think she gave me more than just twelve - I was crying uncontrollably, feeling utterly helpless and as if my entire world consisted of Mistress Joanna's hand on my bottom. When she finished she let me get to my feet. She untied my wrists and asked if I was going to be a good girl from now on.

"Yes Mistress," I curtseyed, still sobbing and desperate to hear a kind word from her to let me know that I wasn't going to be spanked any more.

"Good girl." I almost collapsed with relief, the pain in my bottom still burning but paling into insignificance against the rush of happiness I felt that she thought I was good.

"So Jenny, was it worth being punished to get a kiss from me?"

Another curtsey, another 'Yes Mistress.' She took me in her arms and kissed me roughly. One of her hands found the front of my panties and began to rub gently, causing another erection. The kiss finished and she was still holding my erection as she said. "I can see why Julie wants you to keep that little thing but I still think I'd prefer you without it. Come on."

Three

She led me into the bedroom still gripping my manhood through my panties. Julie had laid a pink satin dress out on the bed and had set a load of makeup on the dresser. I didn't get a chance to see the dress as I was led directly to a seat in front of the dresser mirror. Julie herself was wearing a very sexy French maid's dress in beautiful forest green satin. There was a matching bow in her hair and she was wearing cute white canvas pumps with ribbons that matched her dress as shoelaces. She curtseyed to Mistress Joanna as we entered.

Julie began working on my face, applying makeup as Joanna lounged naked in a large armchair watching, her fingers gently caressing herself between her legs. My head felt like it was stuffed with cotton wool and I was desperately trying to understand everything that was happening but I could see Joanna in the mirror and the sight of her beautiful body was pushing most other thoughts out of my head. Julie looked stunning in her sexy maid costume and the feeling of her satin dress brushing against me as she bustled about putting my makeup on kept me shivering with pleasure. The whole time she worked on me she was talking to me, telling me how pretty I was going to be telling me that I was going to be as beautiful as Mistress Joanna. Every time I tried to pin down a thought about what she was doing to me, her words interrupted it and threw me back into confusion. Why was she putting makeup on me? I wasn't a girl, was I? She was telling me that I was going to become one so maybe that was why. Why was I going to become a girl? Did I want to be a girl or was it just happening and they were helping me? I couldn't remember for sure what I was supposed to be if I wasn't a girl.

"This lipstick looks so pretty on you! You want to look pretty don't you?"

Did I? "I don't know. Why do I want to be pretty?"

"Of course you do. You don't want to be horrible and ugly. Do you?"

"No...but..."

"So you *do* want to be pretty?"

"Yes?"

"Good girl. You like being a pretty girl. You want to be a pretty girl and look like Mistress Joanna don't you? Isn't she the most beautiful person in the world?"

Joanna was smiling as Julie said this and I smiled back at her reflection. "Of course!"

"Then you want to be pretty too, don't you? You want to please us and be pretty for us."

"Yes." My mind grasped this fact as it was about the only thing that didn't slip away immediately. Of course Joanna was beautiful. So was Julie. Why would I want to be any less pretty if they could help me? Looking pretty was a good thing, right?

"Of course you do. You want to look pretty and be a girl like us. You want to please us and obey Mistress Joanna. Horrible ugly boys get their cocks cut off but pretty girls who obey might be allowed to keep them."

That seemed to make sense. I think it was what Mistress Joanna had been saying too. They both seemed very sure about it and I didn't want my cock cut off as I knew that would displease Julie even if it would please Joanna. Didn't Joanna say I would be allowed to keep it because Julie wanted me to? I frowned, trying to remember but as Julie's voice went on and on, hypnotically telling me I was going to be a pretty girl for them, the main thing that I could remember was that I needed to be pretty.

"Yes, I want to be pretty Mistress Julie."

She gasped and I saw Joanna frowning in the mirror. "You call her 'Miss Julie'. You call me 'Mistress'. Remember that, Jenny, unless you want to be spanked again."

"I'm sorry Mistress Joanna. I'm sorry Miss Julie. I do want to be pretty and I don't want to be spanked."

Maybe I *was* becoming a girl. They both certainly seemed to think so. I still wasn't sure that they were right – girls don't have a willy, at least I didn't think so – but they were obviously better able to grasp everything that was happening than I was so the best thing to do was to just trust them.

Julie continued talking as she worked and I fell into a trance. I was getting more and more confused about what was going on. I kept looking back and forth between Julie and Joanna in the mirror, having trouble working out which was which and wondering who that other girl was in the mirror with the red hair and the pink corset. She looked a lot like the twins but I didn't remember seeing her before. She looked just as confused as I felt and I smiled at her to reassure her – Mistress Joanna knew what was going on and as long as we were both good girls, things would be okay. I'm sure that the girl in the mirror didn't want her willy cut off either, if she had one. She smiled back at me.

It was all terribly confusing and as Julie's hypnotic voice continued on I had vague memories of other times when she had talked to me like this while I was under the influence of the pink pills, telling me how much I loved them both and wanted to obey them and that I didn't want to resist anything they did to me. I wondered why she'd ever felt the need to tell me something so obvious.

Eventually Julie finished her work and stood back for Joanna to inspect me.

"Perfect," she declared.

"Thank you Mistress Joanna," curtseyed Julie.

"Don't you think she's done a splendid job, Jenny? Don't you think you look pretty?"

"Do I?" I frowned, not sure how I could tell.

"Yes, very." She gestured towards the mirror and I saw the pretty girl whose name I didn't know again, looking even more like Joanna and Julie in her full makeup and very pretty in her pink corset with the matching bow in her hair.

"But…Is that Jenny?"

"Of course," smiled Julie.

"I thought I was Jenny. Wait, that's not..." I couldn't remember any other name and Jenny sounded right, so was the girl in the mirror called Jenny too? "She's very pretty..."

Joanna and Julie laughed and Julie took my hand and helped me to my feet. Still wondering who this other Jenny was and where she'd gone I was led over to the bed. Julie picked up the pink dress and held it up so that I could see it was a match for hers but in pink satin instead of green.

"You're going to look wonderful in this," she smiled.

"Of course, just like Julie does in hers," agreed Joanna. "Two perfect submissive little maids for me."

"But it's a dress," I said.

"Of course," she smiled indulgently. "You're a girl and girls wear dresses, silly."

"Oh yeah! I forgot," I giggled. What a silly mistake to make.

Julie began helping me into the dress and I wondered if maybe they had made the mistake after all. I didn't remember ever wearing a dress before and surely I would have, if I was a girl? I tried to remember whether girls had willies or not. I wasn't sure that I was a girl but they seemed certain and I had been making a lot of mistakes recently so perhaps some girls had willies and I was one of them. It still didn't seem quite right, surely I wasn't a girl, I was a...m-something? What was the word? As I struggled to complete the thought, Julie slipped my arms into the sleeves and buttoned the dress at the back.

The dress felt strange – lovely, but strange. The soft satin covering my body over the corset and the petticoats and skirt brushing against my legs. I definitely couldn't remember wearing a dress before at all and I'm sure I would have remembered wearing something that felt this nice. Julie's hypnotic voice was still droning on telling me how pretty I looked in my dress and how nice it felt to wear a beautiful dress for Mistress Joanna.

The little puffed sleeves of the dress caught my fascination for a moment and I forgot what I'd been wondering about. Any worries had completely vanished by the time Julie had tied an apron round my waist and started to give me a long, sexy kiss. I was lost in the sensation of her mouth hungrily against mine and her hands all over me through the satin. The rustle of our petticoats brushing against each other and the feel of her gorgeous body inside her own gloriously soft satin dress made it impossible to do anything but submit to her kiss.

I felt a rush of satisfaction as I stiffened in my panties. I had been right – I did have a willy! Some girls must have them after all so obviously I wasn't a…a…whatever the other thing was. I was on the verge of fainting by the time Julie finished kissing me. She turned back to face Joanna, with a huge smile on her face.

"Very good, girls. You look beautiful."

"Thank you Mistress Joanna," curtseyed Julie, elbowing me in the side.

"Thank you Mistress Joanna," I managed, a moment later, attempting to emulate her curtsey. It felt a lot easier in this short, full dress than it did in a nightie or with my hands tied. Oh! The nightie! That was a little like a dress, wasn't it? So I must have worn a dress before. Because I was a girl, not a…a…

Joanna smiled, banishing any further thoughts from my head. "You'll need to practise that curtsey a bit more, Jenny dear. Julie will teach you. Now, dress me please girls."

I managed to remember to curtsey and say "Yes Mistress Joanna" only a fraction of a second slower than Julie did this time. Joanna stood in the middle of the space in the bedroom, gloriously naked as Julie picked up a pair of black satin panties and knelt in front of her. With a frown Julie tugged at the hem of my dress and I realised that I was expected to kneel as well. I did so, still feeling a little strange in the dress and corset with the skirts and petticoats brushing against the backs of my legs as I knelt. Julie leant forward to kiss Joanna's foot. I was getting turned on by the sight and she looked back at me with another frown, reaching up to grab the back of my head and push my face down as well.

I copied Julie, planting gentle kisses on Joanna's foot and kissing my way up her leg while Julie did the same to her other leg. The petticoats brushing against my erection through my panties just made it stiffen even more as I kissed her and caressed her leg with my hands.

Joanna parted her legs slightly as we worked out way up to her thighs, running our hands up and down the backs of them as we kissed the soft, sensitive skin. Julie grabbed the back of my head again and pushed my face between Joanna's legs for me to kiss her there. I moaned in arousal as Joanna did the same. I felt Julie's hand pulling my head back again and I continued kissing Joanna's thigh as Julie took a turn to kiss her between her legs. I glanced up and Joanna had tipped her head back and closed her eyes, breathing heavily as Julie kissed her. Julie moved back to kissing her thighs and pushed my head back between Joanna's legs. I felt Joanna's hand running through my hair and kissed her for a few moments before I felt Julie nudging me out of the way.

"Oh yes," sighed Joanna. "Worship me with your tongues, my beautiful girls."

I saw that Julie was now licking Joanna between her legs, her tongue flicking in and out, lapping at her. Joanna's hand was still on my head and I felt a gentle pressure and obeyed as Julie moved away to let me lick Joanna. After several months of being tied to the bed and using my mouth on her, I knew exactly how she liked to be licked and I was also breathing heavily, the effect of the pink pills magnifying all my sensations and intoxicated by the feel of her clitoris firm against my tongue. I moaned in frustration as she pushed my head away for Julie to take over and desperately kissed her thigh, exasperated that I could no longer be giving her pleasure between her legs.

Before long Julie moved aside and I was licking Joanna again, trying even harder now and desperate to please her after being denied my position between her legs for those moments. I almost cried out in frustration again as she pushed me away for Julie's turn but my frustration was short-lived as she pushed Julie away again after less than a minute. Julie moaned, expressing identical dismay at losing her place as I had felt only moments before. Joanna was breathing more and more heavily now, her breath coming in gasps and whimpers as she swapped our faces between her legs more and more frequently. Julie and I were moaning in anguish and hunger each time we were pushed aside in favour of the other one and we swapped faster and faster, gradually getting into a rhythm of licking Joanna a couple of times before the other one got to lick her a couple of times, back and forth almost fighting each other in our need to feel her against our tongues.

Joanna staggered back a few steps and sat on the bed, opening her legs wide. Julie and I hurriedly crawled over to her, desperate to be the first one to be able to lick her again. I could feel Julie's satin clad body against me, her face next to mine as we kissed and licked Joanna's thighs and clitoris in a frenzy of lust. I heard Joanna gasp loudly and let out a long moan. Both Julie and I dived as close as we could, our tongues almost literally entwining as we both tried to lick Joanna at the same time. Her hands were on our heads holding us there and within a few seconds she was crying out and shuddering beneath our mouths as she came. We carried on licking until she pushed our heads back and collapsed on the bed, gasping for breath.

I was thoroughly turned on and went to stand up, expecting to climb on the bed and for the three of us to continue giving each other orgasms until we were all sated but Julie grabbed me and pulled me back to my knees. We remained kneeling, gazing at Joanna's perfect nakedness as she writhed slowly on the bed before us, recovering from her orgasm. After a couple of minutes she stood on shaky legs and stepped between us, back into the centre of the space in the bedroom. With a contented look on her face she stretched, pushing her arms up high which caused her beautiful breasts to press forwards, making my erection throb even more.

"I think I'm going to love having two maids. That was so much better than just one."

"Thank you Mistress Joanna," we chimed in chorus. I noticed that Julie glared at me for a moment and wondered what I'd done to make her angry. I was trying to be good and follow her lead. She motioned me forwards and we moved over to Joanna, still on our knees. Julie picked up the black satin panties from where she had dropped them. She motioned for me to hold them too and we held them out for Mistress Joanna to step into. I copied Julie in kissing her legs as we pulled them up and into place round her hips.

Julie motioned for me to stay kneeling as she stood and fetched a bra that matched the panties. I stayed where I was, gazing raptly up at Joanna as Julie helped her into the bra, standing behind her and allowing me a magnificent view of Joanna's breasts as the bra cups slipped over them and her breasts nestled into place.

Julie motioned me to stand so I obeyed then followed her lead once more as she adjusted one of Joanna's bra straps and I adjusted the other. "Not too tight, Jenny," she said.

"Yes Miss Julie," I replied.

Julie fetched a suspender belt and fastened it round Joanna's waist. "Tuck the straps through the panties, like this Jenny."

"Yes Miss Julie." I copied what she was doing, still throbbing in my panties and almost trembling as my fingers touched Joanna's thighs. Joanna sat down at the dresser, facing into the room. Julie knelt and slowly rolled a stocking up Joanna's leg and clipped it into place with the suspender strap at the front. She handed me a stocking and I attempted to copy her, not doing it as effortlessly but managing it and still trembling at the touch of Joanna's flesh against mine as my fingers worked at the unfamiliar clasp on the suspender strap.

Joanna stood and turned and, kneeling behind her, Julie and I fastened the rear suspender strap to each stocking top, planting gentle kisses on the backs of her thighs. Julie hauled me to my feet and Joanna sat back down, facing the mirror this time. Julie handed me a hairbrush and I began to gently brush Joanna's long beautiful fiery red curls while Julie carefully applied Joanna's makeup, using the same items she had used on me and that I could see she had used on herself while I had been receiving my spanking in the bathroom.

The last pink pill they'd given me was wearing off a little – not that the effects ever wore off completely – and my thinking a little less muddled. I was lost in the sensations of brushing Joanna's amazing hair and watching Julie work in her sexy dress and the feelings of wearing such a sexy dress myself. I could see in the mirror just how much I looked like Julie and Joanna now. My hair was still straight not curled but my makeup matched perfectly and at a quick glance you'd be sure that I was related to them, although not a twin. I just about understood that the girl I'd been confused about in the mirror earlier had been me. I was slightly relieved to have that cleared up and no longer be worrying that I wasn't sure if I was Jenny or that was someone else they were talking about.

Julie finished her work on Joanna's makeup and I could see that she had been made up exactly the same was as Julie and I. Or rather, we had been made up to look like her.

"How many strokes have you done Jenny?" asked Julie.

I stopped brushing Joanna's hair and looked at her in confusion. "What?"

"How many strokes of the hairbrush? You need to brush Mistress Joanna's hair one hundred times." She was frowning now.

I felt a tear spring to my eyes, "I don't know!" I tried to remember but I hadn't been keeping count at all.

Julie looked furious as she stepped behind me and lifted the back of my dress. "I don't know how many. I didn't know I needed to count."

I felt a sharp smack on my bottom and cried out. This was followed by two more sharp, painful smacks before Julie allowed the hem of my dress to fall.

"Then you'd better make sure you count properly tomorrow."

Crying a little in distress, I tried a curtsey. "Yes Miss Julie. I'm sorry. I'm sorry Mistress Joanna."

Julie still looked angry but Joanna just looked amused as Julie ordered me to kneel and await my next instructions. Trying not to cry any more, I obeyed. I knelt there looking at Joanna with pleading eyes, hoping that she could see how sorry I was. She turned away to let Julie put her earrings in and it felt like my heart was about to burst in despair as I knelt there in my dress, trying not to cry as the pair of them ignored me.

When she finished, Julie curtseyed and moved back half a step while Joanna inspected her work in the mirror. "Perfect as always, Julie my dear. And Jenny hasn't ruined my hair."

"Thank you Mistress Joanna," beamed Julie.

I remained on my knees, watching as Joanna reached out and put her hand under Julie's dress. As if ordered or knowing what was expected, Julie clasped her hands behind her back as Joanna touched her through her panties. They were gazing into each other's eyes as Joanna rubbed Julie between her legs. Julie was gasping and breathing heavily now, much as Joanna had been half an hour earlier as we both licked her. Her breathing was erratic, coming in fits and starts in time with Joanna's hand movements under her dress. I could see that she was having trouble staying upright and my erection was growing again at the sight of Julie looking exactly how Joanna had and the overwhelming desire to feel Joanna's hand under my dress like that. I couldn't take my eyes off them.

Julie staggered slightly and leant back against the dresser, her hands still clasped behind her back and obviously completely at the mercy of Joanna's caresses through her panties. As Joanna continued to rub her, Julie finally unclasped her hands and put them on the dresser behind her to support her as Joanna rubbed her faster. I could feel myself straining against my panties, certain that I was about to pop out and half convinced that I was about to come just from watching what Joanna was doing to her double. I moaned in arousal and frustration that I wasn't being touched like that and Joanna glanced at me with a mischievous smile before looking back at Julie.

Julie gasped again then cried out as she came, still gripping the dresser as Joanna continued to touch her. As she leant against it gulping in air, Joanna removed her hand and smoothed down the front of Julie's dress. Trembling, Julie struggled to stand properly and performed a shaky curtsey. "Thank you Mistress Joanna."

Joanna turned back to me and gestured for me to stand. I did so, elated that I was getting her attention again and breathing heavily in anticipation of her hand going under my dress. Remembering to copy Julie, I clasped my hands behind my back. Joanna smiled and lifted the front of my dress and I moaned softly, wanting her touch through my panties more than anything I had ever wanted in my whole life. "How sweet," she smiled as she studied my erection. "And how presumptuous." She dropped the front of my dress and I moaned again, this time in frustration. "I'm sure Julie will deal with that for you later if you are a good girl." She turned to Julie, "I think young Jenny needs something to keep her from trying to touch that little thing while you start her training, don't you?"

"Yes Mistress Joanna," grinned Julie. As I stood there, hands still clasped behind my back and craving Joanna's touch under my dress, Julie opened a drawer and found what she was looking for. Joanna was playing with the hem of my dress, causing the petticoats to brush infuriatingly gently against the front of my panties.

Julie stepped behind me and I felt her reach round and wrap something round my neck. With a glance in the mirror I realised that she was fastening a pink satin and white lace collar that was a perfect match for my maid dress. I felt her lacing it up at the back, feeling a little trapped. It wasn't too tight but I could feel that it was secure. Two long wide pink satin ribbons hung from the collar and she turned me to face her, eliciting another moan of frustration as my erection moved away from the tantalisingly close promise of Mistress Joanna's hand. Julie took one of my hands and tied the satin ribbon around my wrist, again not too tight but tight enough that I wouldn't be able to slip my hand out and secure enough that I wouldn't be able to undo the knot with just one hand. She did the same for my other hand and stepped back with a huge grin.

"That should stop any inappropriate touching of herself until you give her permission, Mistress Joanna."

The two ribbons were long enough for me to reach my hands to my waist but they were not long enough for me to be able to reach to lift the front of my dress or touch myself through my panties. This was proven to me when Joanna stood to inspect me and ordered me to try. I moaned in frustration at the raging erection I had and being ordered to try to touch it without any real hope of being able to do so. The best I could manage was to gradually bunch the front of my dress up but with the length of the ribbons and the full skirt and petticoats, touching myself through my panties was impossible.

Joanna giggled when she saw the erection in my panties and my frustrated scrabbling at the front of my dress

My hands went to the back of the collar but it was instantly obvious that there was no way I'd be able to untie it without being able to see what I was doing. Julie slapped my hands away from the collar and I mumbled, "Sorry Miss Julie," as she tidied the front of my dress and my apron that I'd rucked up. I tried to press my erection against her as she did so but she wouldn't let me and lifted the back of my dress for two more sharp spanks which instantly stopped me from misbehaving.

"Perfect," smiled Joanna.

Julie went to one of the wardrobes and pulled out a dress. She brought it over and ordered me to help her. She had selected a heavy black silk wrapover dress and we held a side of it each while Joanna held her arms for us to slip it onto her. We wrapped the dress round her and Julie tied it at the back. Joanna sat back down to allow Julie and I to kneel and each slip a black patent leather court shoe onto one of her feet. I remained kneeling while Julie stood and fastened an expensive watch round the slender wrist that Joanna held out for her.

She stood and glanced at the watch. It's a bit late for breakfast so I will take an early lunch in the conservatory in half an hour."

"Yes Mistress Joanna," curtseyed Julie.

"Yes Mistress Joanna," I echoed from my knees in front of her.

Joanna caressed my face with her hand, gave Julie a long French kiss and swept out of the room.

Julie gestured for me to stand and I struggled to my feet, unable to reach my hands out to help. Without a word she twirled her finger, ordering me to turn round. "Yes Miss Julie," I said as I did so, attempting a curtsey without being able to grasp the hem of my dress.

I felt her lift the back of my dress. She spanked me hard and I yelped. "How many strokes of the hairbrush are you supposed to give to Mistress Joanna's hair?" she asked.

I yelped as she smacked me again. "One hundred strokes Miss Julie! I'm sorry Miss Julie. I didn't know, I'll do it properly next time."

She smacked me again. "You'd better or you will be getting one spank for every stroke you miss and if you completely fail to count then it will be one hundred spanks." She smacked me again. "I will let you off this first time as you didn't know but you should have asked."

"Yes Miss Julie, thank you Miss Julie. I'm sorry I upset you both."

She rearranged the back of my dress and I felt relief, both that I wasn't about to get such a spanking but also that she didn't seem too angry. The thought of upsetting either of my two beautiful women was too distressing.

She stepped back around in front of me and I gasped as her hand went under the front of my dress. My erection was still throbbing and it was straining for her touch. Her hand didn't touch me through my panties though, she just fluffed the dress and petticoats, keeping her hand there and making me moan in frustration as she teased me. I desperately wanted her to touch me but I knew that I had been a naughty girl so far and didn't want any more spanks so I just moaned softly as she played with the front of my dress, the index finger of her other hand on her chin as she pondered. "Once we've prepared lunch I will start to show you what your chores are." Her hand was still fiddling with my petticoats and I occasionally felt the lightest touch of her fingertips against my thigh but not through my panties. It was driving me wild and I could hardly concentrate on what she was saying.

Four

Julie made me sit down so that she could place a pair of canvas shoes on my feet. They were identical to hers but had pink ribbons for laces instead of green. With my wrists attached to my collar I couldn't reach to tie them myself. Afterwards she led me downstairs and we began to prepare Mistress Joanna's lunch.

It was clear that Julie was in charge, despite also being Joanna's maid. I tried to do everything she ordered but I was completely unable to concentrate properly and made silly mistakes. Each time I did Julie lifted the back of my dress to deliver two hard spanks, making me yelp and beg forgiveness. I was trying to do my best but everything was so hard to remember! I was glad that Julie was there though, she seemed to know exactly what needed doing and gave me detailed instructions. I didn't think I could have managed it on my own and the last thing I wanted to do was ruin Mistress Joanna's lunch. The passionate kisses from Julie didn't help my concentration much, and neither did her constant caresses of me through my soft satin dress or putting her hand under the skirt to caress my bottom through my panties or touch me through the front of them to ensure that I was still hard.

We served Mistress Joanna's lunch in the conservatory as ordered. Julie sat on Joanna's lap to feed her, squirming in pleasure and giggling at Joanna's hand under her dress. I stood by to pass things to Julie, my erection throbbing in my panties at the sight of what Joanna was doing to Julie and desperately wishing that it was me sat on her lap being fondled through my panties. I groaned in frustration at the erection and my inability to touch it, even slightly. As I watched Joanna bring Julie to another orgasm by touching her under her maid dress I wanted nothing more than to prove to Mistress Joanna what a good maid I could be if it would mean that I would get the same treatment from her.

When she finished eating, Mistress Joanna dismissed us both and Julie led me out of the conservatory to the kitchen where we were allowed to eat our own lunches. I served Julie her food and we sat and ate, with her telling me what our chores were for the rest of the day. After lunch she started instructing me in my chores. My erection was still aching but there was nothing I could do about it and Julie was obviously enjoying herself teasing me and keeping me erect and frustrated as she ordered me about. I tried my hardest to follow all her instructions, the only thought in my head being that I needed to be a good maid for Mistress Joanna if I wanted to please her.

Joanna spent the day relaxing and being pampered by her maids, seemingly enjoying the sight of me being trained by Julie to obey her. As she watched me dusting the living room where she lounged on the sofa with a glass of wine, she was touching herself between her legs as Julie gave me orders. She could see that I was stealing glances at her and moaned in apparent arousal as Julie decided that I had missed a bit and once again lifted the back of my skirt to deliver two hard spanks. Joanna was breathing heavily and rubbing herself faster as she watched me beg forgiveness and promise to try harder. I was mortified that I had made another mistake but pleased that Mistress Joanna was enjoying herself.

We cleaned the kitchen, the living room and one of the bathrooms then started preparing dinner. While it was cooking, Mistress Joanna decided to make an inspection of our work. We followed her round the house, standing obediently to attention as she checked everything we had done and either approved or pointed out where things weren't good enough. Julie glared angrily at me every time Mistress Joanna pointed out something that wasn't to her satisfaction. Eventually she finished her inspection and ordered us to follow her to her study.

When we entered Julie curtseyed then knelt and I followed suit. Joanna sat down in her armchair and studied us both. "I hope your work won't be quite so slapdash tomorrow," she said eventually.

"Sorry Mistress Joanna," said Julie. "Jenny is having trouble learning. I think she needs to be punished."

I gasped and Julie gave me a mischievous grin.

"Yes, she does," agreed Joanna, "but it's not entirely her fault. I entrusted you with her training and you've also let me down. Bend over my desk."

Julie glared at me but stood up, curtseyed and said, "Yes Mistress Joanna," as she obediently bent over Joanna's desk. Joanna stood and went over to her. Silently she lifted the back of Julie's dress and delivered three sharp spanks. Julie gasped at each one but did nothing to resist. Despite being certain that I was next, I couldn't help but be aroused at the sight of the gorgeous Julie being spanked by the equally gorgeous Mistress Joanna. Kneeling like this I could almost but not quite touch my erection with my hands tied to my collar and I covertly tried to touch myself through my panties as I watched Joanna spank Julie.

I was still straining to touch myself through the front of my dress as Joanna tugged the hem of Julie's dress back down and allowed her to stand. Julie curtseyed and said, "Thank you Mistress Joanna." Joanna stroked her face then gave her a long passionate kiss.

I was thoroughly aroused but unable to do anything about it. Finally they finished kissing and Joanna sat back down. "You may punish her now," she said to Julie. Julie gasped and her eyes were twinkling as she said an excited, "Thank you Mistress Joanna!" and beckoned me to stand. I struggled to my feet and attempted a curtsey.

Julie gave me a stern look and ordered me to bend over the desk. I wanted to refuse, scared of the spanking I was about to receive but knowing that there was nothing I could do about it. A tear rolled down my cheek as I looked imploringly at Mistress Joanna, even more horrified at what she must think of me being such a bad maid than at the thought of my punishment. "I'm sorry Mistress Joanna," I cried as I obeyed Julie and bent over the desk. "I'll try to be a good maid for you. I'm sorry."

"I know you will, Jenny darling. Otherwise you'll be having your little willy cut off, won't you? Don't worry, I'm not angry really, I just want to see you getting spanked." She lounged back in her chair and hooked one leg over the arm. As I felt Julie lift the back of my dress I saw Joanna lift the front of her dress at the same time and start touching herself through her black panties.

"This is for getting me in trouble," hissed Julie and she spanked me hard three times. Mistress Joanna gasped and grinned in time with my yelps as Julie's hand came down hard on my bottom.

"And this is for disappointing Mistress Joanna." She spanked me several more times, with me begging forgiveness and incoherently promising to behave myself. "You want to be a good girl, don't you?" asked Julie, raining several more hard smacks down on my bottom. Through my tears I could see Joanna rubbing herself through her panties.

"I want to be a good girl," I sobbed as Julie continued spanking me. I was sure she was spanking me a lot harder than Mistress Joanna had spanked her just now and it was the pain making me cry as much as the humiliation and shame at being so naughty.

"You want to be a beautiful girl too, don't you? You want to look just like Mistress Joanna and be loved by us."

"Oh yes!" I cried, desperate for their love and wanting to please them more than anything. "Please teach me how to be a good girl and to be like you!"

Joanna was gasping louder now and her hand had slipped inside her panties.

"Good girl," said Julie and started to caress my stinging bottom instead, making me feel a wave of gratitude towards her for ending the spanking. She was moaning now as she caressed my bottom through my panties. "You're going to be so beautiful just like Mistress Joanna. You're going to be perfect just like her."

"Don't stop spanking her!" gasped Mistress Joanna, rubbing frantically between her legs now.

I cried out as Julie smacked me again and Joanna gasped loudly as I cried out.

"Again!"

Julie raised her hand and I started begging her not to but to no avail as her hand came down hard on my bottom and the tears started again. The smacks came faster and faster now, in time with Mistress Joanna's cries and despite the stinging I was getting aroused at seeing her and knowing that she was excited by seeing me being spanked, which was infinitely preferable to being ignored by her or her being angry with me.

Finally she came loudly, bucking on her chair. Julie stopped spanking me and began caressing me again, soothing my sore bottom. I cried tears of relief now, at the end to the pain and the elation that Mistress Joanna was no longer angry with me.

"Oh my beautiful girls!" gasped Joanna breathlessly.

Julie straightened my dress and helped me upright and we stood watching as Mistress Joanna regained her composure and straightened her own dress. "I think young Jenny has learned her lesson, don't you Julie?"

Julie curtseyed, "Yes Mistress Joanna." She smiled at me and I felt another rush of relief that she no longer seemed angry with me.

"I think she deserves a kiss."

"Yes Mistress Joanna," Julie gently wiped the last of my tears away and put her arms round my neck. I put my hands on her waist, thrilled at the feeling of her amazing body beneath the sexy satin dress. I felt her breasts pressing against me as she pulled me close and kissed me passionately. I melted into her embrace as her tongue pushed its way into my mouth and her groin pressed against mine, the feeling of her against my erection making me light-headed after the hours of frustration and our soft satin skirts and petticoats mingling and caressing my thighs sending shivers of sensual pleasure through me. Submissively I responded to her long kiss, my bottom still stinging but the memory of the spanking fading rapidly as my beautiful lover kissed me and I could see Mistress Joanna gently caressing herself through the bodice of her dress as she watched us.

My knees were weak when Joanna finished kissing me and curtseyed to Mistress Joanna. I almost felt like fainting but managed with some effort to remain upright. Joanna stood and came over to us, her hand caressing my face as she gave Julie a passionate kiss then did the same to me. All I felt was joy as she kissed me and everything seemed alright again.

"You see Jenny? All you need to do is obey me and I'll make you happier than you can possibly imagine. You're not a boy any more. You're going to be my double, just like Julie and you're going to thank me for making you perfect."

"Oh yes Mistress Joanna," I sighed in rapt adoration.

She smiled, "Call me when dinner is ready."

"Yes Mistress Joanna," curtseyed Julie. I managed a clumsy curtsey as she left the room.

Julie gave me another long kiss. "Do you think you can manage to behave yourself this evening Jenny?"

"Yes Miss Julie."

"Good girl," she patted my cheek. "You can serve dinner for both of us. Follow me."

She led me up to their bedroom and I helped her out of her maid dress and into a dark green silk dress that was a match for the one that Mistress Joanna was wearing. She gave me another long kiss and reached under the front of my dress, making me moan as she touched my erection. "I'm sure you'll be allowed to enjoy this if you are a good maid this evening."

"I promise!" I blurted out.

She smiled, "Good girl. I'm sure you don't want to give Mistress Joanna any reason to get rid of it. I would be very unhappy with you if she decided to punish you by taking it away."

"I don't want it cut off," I gasped. "I'll be good." Why did they both keep talking about having my willy cut off? That wasn't something that happened was it? I still couldn't remember for sure if I was even supposed to have one in the first place. Was having it cut off something that happened to every girl? No, that wasn't right…was it? I felt a little dizzy trying to work it all out.

She led me back down to the kitchen and told me what needed doing next. She sat and supervised me as I followed her instructions as well as I could, determined to be a good maid as I didn't want another spanking, and didn't want my willy cut off instead of having them touching it this evening. Julie seemed pleased at how obedient and eager to please I was.

When everything was ready, Julie sent me to summon Mistress Joanna. I went to her study and knocked on the door. "Enter," she called out. I checked that my dress was straight and opened the door. With a curtsey I said, "Dinner is ready now Mistress Joanna."

"Thank you Jenny," she smiled.

I beamed with happiness.

In the dining room, Julie instructed me as I served their meals and poured drinks for them. When they had both been served Joanna gave me permission to sit and eat. I thanked her happily, glad at being able to eat with them and quickly obeying if they wanted me to pass something or pour more wine.

After our meal, I cleared the things from the dining room and Mistress Joanna retired to her study again while Julie followed me to the kitchen. She made me take one of the pink pills then sat and watched me, giving me more instructions as I cleared up the kitchen. Gradually I could feel the effects of the pill coming on and I could feel my concentration slipping. I was nearly in tears as I realised that I couldn't quite remember what I was supposed to be doing and almost begged Miss Julie to remind me.

With an indulgent smile, she reminded me and as I struggled to complete the task she had given me I could hear her hypnotic voice telling me how much I loved being their maid and how happy it made me to serve them and how badly I wanted to be a beautiful girl just like them.

After a while I felt Julie touch my arm. I stopped what I was doing and turned to face her, wondering if I had done something wrong but she was smiling at me. "Come on Jenny, I think that's enough housework for one day." She took my hand and I followed her upstairs to the exercise room. She untied my wrists and helped me out of my maid dress and the corset. I sighed with relief but felt oddly insecure without it.

Julie made me lie down on the massage table and tied me to it again. Joanna reappeared partway through Julie massaging me and helped out and I lay there moaning softly at the wonderful sensation of being touched by both of them. They turned me onto my back to continue the massage and I was fully erect but neither of them were touching me there, although Julie was looking at it with a hungry glint in her eye. I lay there in a trance as she talked on and on about how pretty I was going to be and how obedient I was and how I was a girl and always had been. I felt confusion again – why would she say that? I couldn't remember if I had always been a girl but I also couldn't remember what else I might have been if I hadn't always been a girl. I struggled to remember, wondering once more if girls had willies or not and why I had one.

After what felt like hours of being pummelled by them I was untied and taken through to the bedroom where Julie helped me into a short pink nightie then tied my wrists back into the ribbons attached to my collar. They lay me down on the bed and climbed on with me, kneeling each side of me and taking one of my hands and putting it under their dress so I could touch them through their panties. I moaned in arousal as they started kissing over me, my hands rubbing them and their hands caressing me through my nightie and on my bare thighs. I groaned in frustration every time one of their hands moved against my pink satin panties without properly touching my erection, teasing me. Julie came first, her thighs clamping against my hand. I continued rubbing Mistress Joanna as Julie rubbed me through the crotch of my panties, still not touching my erection and moving her hand every time I tried to move my hips to bring it under her palm.

Joanna came soon after and her hand was stroking me through my nightie as she gave Julie long kiss then leaned down to give me a long kiss. She was looking right in my eyes as her hand gently touched my erection. "Good girl. I will let you keep this a while longer. Do you want to keep it?"

"Yes please Mistress Joanna," I sighed happily.

She smiled and looked at Julie. "Do you think Jenny should be allowed to keep her little willy?"

"Yes please Mistress Joanna," replied Julie. "Can I touch it properly now please?"

"Hmmm." Joanna looked back down at me. "Would you like her to touch it Jenny?"

"Oh yes! Yes please Mistress Joanna!"

"Hmmm. Will you be a good girl tomorrow when I have someone here to help you look even more like me?"

"Yes Mistress Joanna. I will be a good girl. I want to look like you, you're so beautiful!"

She beamed at me, making my heart leap. "Promise?"

"Yes Mistress Joanna, I promise. Please let her touch me."

She looked stern all of a sudden and I wondered if I had displeased her. "I take promises *very* seriously Jenny. Any trouble from you tomorrow and I will be arranging a trip to the clinic for you." She caressed my balls gently, making me moan. "We don't need these and I'll get rid of them if you make me angry. Understood?"

I felt a tiny bit of fear but was also desperate to please her and desperate to for Julie to touch my erection as it was aching and I needed release. "I understand Mistress Joanna, I'll be a good girl." I was still confused and wasn't sure what she meant about getting rid of them but I was happy that she smiled at me.

She climbed off the bed and I saw her start to remove her dress but everything was suddenly blasted from my mind as Julie started to rub me through my panties. I closed my eyes and moaned in ecstasy as she touched me. I felt her pull the front of my panties down and gasped as I felt her gorgeous lips on my erection. I was paralysed, unable to think or move or do anything but lay there as she kissed and licked me until I exploded in her mouth with a loud cry.

Five

I awoke the next morning to Julie kissing me on the lips and rubbing me through the front of my nightie. I moaned happily and returned the kiss. She pulled back and whispered, "Shh. Don't wake Mistress Joanna."

I glanced over to see Mistress Joanna fast asleep. Both she and Julie had changed into nighties that matched the one I was wearing, in black and green satin respectively. Julie helped me climb off the bed then untied my wrists from the satin ribbons and unfastened the collar. She popped one of the little pink pills into my mouth and led me through to the bathroom where we shared a long kiss before removing our nighties and panties and walking into the shower together. The effects of the pill began to make themselves felt and I was awash with pleasure at the feeling of the hot water splashing against my smooth skin and the touches and kisses we shared as we soaped each other and washed each other's hair.

Julie pressed me back against the wall of the shower room and kissed me roughly, her tongue forcing its way into my mouth and her hand rubbing my erection as she pressed against me and I felt it slip into her. I was gasping as she pulled back saying, "We mustn't get too carried away. I just wanted to make sure your little willy was pleased to see me."

I stood there gasping for breath and hard as a rock as she gave me a mischievous smile and exited the shower.

I was still hard as we dried ourselves and went back to the bedroom to find Mistress Joanna awake but still lying in bed. "Good morning girls," she smiled.

Naked, both Julie and I curtsied and replied, "Good morning Mistress Joanna."

"We have visitors today so you girls can go prepare breakfast while I shower. You'll have to get your chores done quicker than usual so no misbehaving. I am *not* in a forgiving mood today." Joanna glanced at my obvious erection. "I do hope you can be trusted to behave yourself today Jenny? Don't forget you promised and what your punishment will be if you displease me."

The pill had left me little confused as usual so I couldn't quite remember what she had said about today but if Mistress Joanna said that I had promised to be good then I must have. All I wanted to do was please her anyway. I didn't want to be punished. I couldn't quite remember what she said the punishment would be. I glanced down at my erection, struggling to remember. Something about my willy? I was distracted by wondering if the hair down there had always been pink. I was still struggling to recall the conversation yesterday when Julie hissed at me to stop daydreaming.

Quickly, Julie laced me into my pink corset and we dressed in our sexy maid outfits as Joanna watched happily. Julie picked up the collar but Joanna said, "I think Jenny can be trusted to be a good girl today without that, in the interests of getting her chores done quickly. Can I trust you to be a good girl Jenny?"

I smiled and curtseyed, "Yes Mistress Joanna, of course I will be a good girl." I felt a sense of relief – the collar had made it awkward to do some things yesterday and it felt good to know that Mistress Julie trusted me. I *wanted* to be a good girl and prove to her how much I loved her.

"Good." Her smile lit up the room and almost made me swoon at the beauty of it. "Because we can so easily get rid of those silly little balls if you find them too much of a distraction from being a good girl."

I curtseyed but frowned, not sure what she was talking about. I hadn't seen any balls. Did they have a tennis court here or something? I supposed the grounds around the house might be large enough. And how would balls stop me being a good girl? I was still trying to work it all out as Julie grabbed my hand and pulled me from the room.

My mind was its usual fuzzy mess from the pink pill as Julie and I prepared breakfast and I was glad of her constant instructions. All the while we worked she was telling me how pretty I was and how much I wanted to be a perfect obedient maid and how happy I was going to be as a girl. I didn't think she needed to keep telling me things that were so obvious but her talking and her caresses through my dress and the way her hand kept going under the skirt made me feel pretty and kept me hard in my panties.

Mistress Joanna came down for breakfast wearing a beautiful long black satin and lace dressing gown and sat with a pleased smile on her face as she watched us work. Her voice joined in with Julie's telling me how perfect I was going to be as a girl and how happy I would be if I obeyed her every command and I felt like I was about to orgasm in my panties from the overwhelming sensuousness of it all.

After breakfast we followed Mistress Joanna back upstairs and the two of us dressed her again, repeating our performance of yesterday, kissing and licking her until she came. We dressed her in a beautiful white satin blouse and black knee-length pencil skirt then she instructed Miss Julie in what makeup she wanted today as I brushed her hair. Fortunately Julie sternly reminded me to count how many times I brushed her hair, although it was a struggle to concentrate well enough to keep count as I kept being distracted by how beautiful they both were and how amazing Mistress Joanna looked in the mirror, having her hair brushed by a pretty maid in a lovely pink dress who looked a lot like her while an equally gorgeous maid in green satin worked on her makeup.

Once we had finished preparing Mistress Joanna, I was taken into the exercise room and stripped and tied to the massage table. "Just because we're busy today is no reason to neglect your figure training Jenny," said Mistress Joanna as she and Julie gave me another pummelling.

Back in my corset and maid dress I went to help Julie tidy the breakfast things away and rush through some of our chores. I could tell that she was in a rush because she was spending less time touching or kissing me and was very quick to lift the back of my dress to deliver two or three sharp spanks whenever I did something wrong. I was doing my best to concentrate on what I was being ordered to do and almost burst into tears of shame each time I forced Julie to spank me, knowing that I had disappointed her and made her angry. The last thing I wanted was for her to be spanked again for my misbehaviour!

Soon after we'd prepared lunch, Julie gave me another pink pill and then Mistress Joanna's visitors arrived. She whispered a harsh, "If you do *anything* to embarrass me in front of my guests, you will be severely punished," and went to greet them at the door. Julie went with her, leaving me in the hallway, not sure what to do and worried that I would do something to make Mistress Joanna unhappy.

There were two visitors. Both women. One was a statuesque woman of about forty with raven black hair and piercing blue eyes. The other was a startlingly cute blonde in her twenties. Mistress Joanna greeted them with kisses while Julie took their coats. I stayed standing where I was, still too nervous to risk doing anything wrong and waiting to be told what to do.

Mistress Joanna led them towards me saying," And this is Jenny." I performed a nervous curtsey as the two women studied me.

"Step forward, girl," ordered the dark haired lady. "Let me get a proper look at you."

I made another curtsey, "Yes Miss," and took a step forward, glancing at Mistress Joanna who smiled at my obedience and nodded slightly. The lady ordered me to turn round slowly and I obeyed.

"Hmmm..." she said. "You've done a very good job of selecting him, Joanna. I would never have believed that you could do to a boy what you did to Julie but he's definitely got potential. I'll need to take a proper look at him."

I gasped. A boy! That's what I was, wasn't it? Not a girl! Boys had willies, not girls. Is that why Mistress Joanna kept talking about cutting my willy off? Because I wasn't supposed to have one if I was a girl? Or was I really a girl like Mistress Joanna and Miss Julie kept insisting and they were only so concerned about my willy because it might make people think I was a boy when I wasn't one?

"You can take a closer look at *her* after lunch."

"Of course. I apologise. How is the conditioning going? Is she responding well?"

I was in a daze, totally unsure what to think or what I was and not understanding what they were talking about now. I looked at Mistress Joanna again, desperate for some reassurance and for her to tell me if I was a girl or a...a...the word was slipping away again.

What was that other thing? The thing that this lady had just mistaken me for?

Mistress Joanna didn't notice my pleading look, she was still talking to this lady, whoever she was.

"She's certainly been a lot less difficult so far than Julie was at first. I've had to spank her a couple of times but to be honest, one of those times was definitely more for fun than punishment. I think she's having a little trouble grasping exactly what is going to happen to her…willy…if she displeases me too much or I get bored but I actually think that is just an indicator of how well she is responding to the pills and conditioning. And perhaps that will make it easier to get rid of it without her relapsing at all."

The dark haired lady laughed, "You're probably right. At least you know her attitude is real, not just out of fear. How long *have* you been conditioning her now?"

"Oh, about four months."

"Wonderful. So the conditioning is probably already permanent."

"Quite likely, but with another couple of months of conditioning she'll be perfect. It took me almost a year to get Julie to properly submit to me and another six months or so on top of that for her to accept the physical changes and the fact that Kelly was gone. Jenny here was completely under my spell within a month and accepted her new hair and makeup and a maid dress with barely a squeak. Frankly, I think I could have moved her forward like this a couple of months ago if it had been convenient."

Finally Mistress Joanna glanced at me and my heart leapt at the look of love and pride on her face. I still didn't really understand what they were talking about but that didn't matter now I knew that Mistress Joanna was happy with me.

"Of course, Julie helping to condition her has made it a lot easier than doing it all myself like I had to the first time."

"I'm not surprised. And it was Julie's idea to do this to a…to someone like Jenny, wasn't it? It's fascinating that the pills seem to be helping you induce gender dysphoria. Is there any associated body dysmorphia?"

Mistress Joanna smiled, "I'm working on it. The start of breasts doesn't seem to be bothering her at all and I want her to be accepting when I decide to have other things removed."

They began to move off down the hallway, continuing their incomprehensible discussion. Not sure what to do I stayed where I was, sure that Mistress Joanna or Miss Julie would let me know what was expected of me. I glanced round and the blonde lady was looking at me with a smile on her face.

"You're going to be very pretty when I've finished with you. You'll be perfect."

I smiled and bobbed a curtsey, "Thank you, Miss." She turned and followed Mistress Joanna and the other lady.

Julie reappeared and gestured for me to follow. "Come on Jenny, we need to serve lunch for Mistress Joanna and her guests."

"Yes Miss Julie," I curtseyed automatically. She too smiled at my obedience and my heart leapt again. I wasn't really sure who these two visitors where or what was going on but it felt good to be doing my best to be a good girl and obey the instructions of Joanna and Julie. All I wanted to do was to please the two most beautiful, sexy, wonderful women in the history of the world.

I was on cloud 9 as I helped Julie serve lunch, ecstatic that both Mistress Joanna and Miss Julie were happy with me. It was the best feeling ever, knowing that I pleased them and it made me feel safe and secure to be receiving clear instructions from Miss Julie so I didn't have to worry about getting something wrong. Their smiles and the look of love in their eyes, the feel of my beautiful satin dress swishing about my thighs as I served lunch, knowing that I was a good girl. It all made me feel special and pretty and the confusion as to who or what I was vanished utterly. I was Jenny, I was a girl and Joanna and Julie were helping me to be even more perfect, like Joanna had helped Julie before me. I felt like bawling my eyes out in gratitude.

After lunch it was decided that it was time for Dr Carol (as I had found out the dark haired lady was called) to examine me properly. I wasn't sure what that meant or why she needed to do so but if it was what Mistress Joanna wanted then I was happy to go along with it.

The women took me to the exercise room where Julie helped me out of my maid dress and corset. I lay on my back on the massage table and Julie tied my wrists above my head to the bar at the top of the table while Mistress Joanna strapped my ankles to the stirrups and spread my legs wide for Dr Carol to examine me.

While the other three women watched, Dr Carol walked slowly round the table, examining me from every angle before prodding my chest and touching my nipples. "She's definitely got the right frame to match yours," she said to Mistress Joanna. The hormones will help but I'm sure she will need some work done."

She continued prodding and poking me in various places. "Yes...if you keep up the massage and use of a corset, I'm sure you'll get her to an acceptable figure."

Soon enough she was standing between my legs. She untied the ribbons holding my panties on and pulled the front of them down to examine me thoroughly. Tied to the table as I was, I couldn't see properly but could feel her hands between my legs, cupping my balls and my cock.

"I assume that all...this...is going at some point?"

I heard Julie gasp and turned my head to see her looking unhappy and beginning to plead with Mistress Joanna. "You said I could keep it!" she beseeched.

Keep what? I wondered. Dr Carol was examining me, not Julie. What could Miss Julie be worried about losing? I felt sorry for her and wanted to comfort her but I didn't know what to say as I didn't really understand what the problem was.

Joanna waved Julie to silence and responded to Dr Carol, "I told Julie that she could keep it for a while but yes, I'll probably get bored with it sooner or later. No matter how much Jenny looks like me, I'll always know that is there, spoiling the perfection."

"Please Mistress Joanna!" begged Julie. Joanna waved her to silence again and Julie obeyed instantly although she didn't look happy.

Dr Carol turned to Mistress Joanna, "Well I can help with an orchiectomy or a penectomy. In fact, if you wanted me to fix him now, I have the things I need with me and could do it with a local anaesthetic. Not a full removal of course, just a tiny incision here," I felt her fingertip touch me between my legs again, "a couple of snips and a few stitches and you won't need to use anti-androgens on him any more."

I was confused again now. Who was this 'him' that Dr Carol was talking about? And snip and stitch what? On him? I thought they were discussing me? Had I missed a part of the conversation somehow? I tried to make sense of it but there was none to be found. I forgot about it quickly anyway when I noticed that Julie's face had changed from one of pleading to one of excitement.

"You could do that without...damaging anything?"

"Easily. And the female hormones would have a much better effect. It wouldn't harm anything, just leave them useless and empty. He'll probably be uncomfortable down there for a few days but nothing worse than that." Dr Carol looked from Julie to Joanna, "Of course, if you want a full vaginoplasty then you'll need a specialist."

"I have one. Along with a selection of photographs and documents that will encourage him to do a very good, very discreet job of it if I decide to."

Julie was hugging Mistress Joanna's arm now. "Please let her do that now! Make her do the..." she made a scissors gesture with her fingers. I just stared at Julie, completely lost as to what the topic of conversation had moved onto now. Hopefully nobody would ask my opinion so I wouldn't have to embarrass myself. All I knew was that Miss Julie obviously wanted something badly so I hoped that she would get her wish. Mistress Joanna was looking aroused by the conversation too so hopefully she would agree.

Mistress Joanna looked thoughtful and Julie looked desperately hopeful. I just drank in the site of the beautiful Mistress Joanna and her equally beautiful double, wondering what I had done to deserve the love of two such gorgeous, incredible women. If only I could be as beautiful and perfect to them as they were to me.

"No. No, I think we'll keep her intact for now."

"Please don't Mistress Joanna! Please let her do this to Jenny! The thought is turning me on so much!"

Mistress Joanna looked irritated with Julie, who immediately looked apologetic and fell into silence.

"No. I'd like to complete her conditioning first. The thought is turning me on too but I'd rather get all that," she waved a hand in the general direction of between my legs, "done in one go. Or even better, have her beg me for it or do it as a punishment."

Dr Carol shrugged, "Your call. I'd be happy to do it whenever you change your mind."

She carried on examining me then took a couple of blood samples. I didn't understand any of the conversation she had with Mistress Joanna about it. Something about monitoring hormone levels. Eventually the three women left the room, still discussing whatever it was they had been talking about this whole time.

Julie retied my panties then untied my ankles and wrists to help me back into my corset and maid dress. She was pouting about something. I asked what was wrong and she stared at me for a moment. "You really don't understand, do you? Those pills are amazing."

I looked confused.

"It sort of makes me wish that Joanna had been able to use them on me at the time. Just the thought of how helpless I'd have been, how quickly she could have had such power over me. All the time I wasted resisting her, too scared to give up being imperfect little Kelly…"

I gaped, completely at a loss for words or understanding.

She shook her head, "Don't worry your pretty little head about it. Mistress Joana is in charge and she'll make all the decisions for you, so you don't have to think or fret. Just concentrate on being a good girl and everything will be fine."

I smiled in relief. "Thank you Miss Julie. I love you and I hope Mistress Joanna changes her mind about what you were asking her for."

She gave me a surprised look then a long kiss then led me to a room I hadn't seen before. It was apparently some sort of guest bedroom where the blonde woman – Susan – had set up various items around a chair with a plastic cover over it. Mistress Joanna was at in a large armchair chatting to Dr Carol.

Julie made me sit on the chair and Susan fastened a cape round my neck, covering my maid dress.

"Okay Jenny," said Susan, "I'm going to make you pretty. You want to be pretty, don't you? As pretty as Joanna and Julie?"

I giggled, "I could never be that pretty, could I?"

"I'll do my best. Don't you think you're pretty already?"

I glanced at myself in the mirror. I guess I did look pretty, because I looked a lot like Joanna and Julie already but compared to their perfection, I was nothing. An imperfect imitation. I frowned. Something wasn't quite right, like I didn't deserve to be as pretty as Joanna and Julie or perhaps wasn't *supposed* to be pretty like them. I shrugged - Maybe I was just starting to see why Mistress Joanna was so adamant about making me more perfect, like her.

I still had the odd notion, somewhere deep down inside me, that I shouldn't be feeling this way but that made no sense. What girl wouldn't literally kill to be as beautiful as Mistress Joanna and Miss Julie? The niggling feeling inside grew a little and there was a word on the tip of my tongue that I couldn't quite recall, a word that meant not-a-girl, a word for someone who wouldn't want to be pretty.

I struggled to remember but I couldn't focus on what it was I was even struggling to remember. Then Julie was there next to me, telling me how pretty I was, what a good maid I'd been today and how I loved being a girl and how nice my satin maid dress felt and how happy it made me to please Mistress Joanna. On and on, knocking all other thought out of my head and putting me in a near trance, hardly able to comprehend anything except her voice and those amazing eyes staring at mine in the mirror.

I was in a daze as Susan began to work on me. I don't know how long I sat in that chair – it felt like it could have been mere seconds or it could have been aeons. I was vaguely aware of what she was doing but it was like watching it happen to someone else, seeing a pretty young woman in the mirror with a marked resemblance to Joanna and Julie becoming more like them both, becoming more perfect.

I sat there, lost in the effects of the pill and Julie's voice and blissful confusion as Susan worked on my hair, cutting it and giving me curls to match Joanna's; plucking my eyebrows and tinting them to match those of the women I loved; piercing my ears with little silver studs that had pink sapphires, to match the emerald studs that Julie was wearing and the black diamond ones in Joanna's ears; applying long false fingernails in a beautiful shade of pink; injecting something into my lips, telling me it would help shape them to be more like Joanna's, lining my eyes with something that would be permanent and finally, completing my makeup to match Joanna's and Julie's.

I stared in the mirror as Susan removed the cape, wondering why I could see Julie's face in the mirror and why she had put on my pink maid dress instead of her green one. My confusion increased as I felt hands on my shoulder then an identical face appeared next to the one in the mirror, wearing a green satin dress and I couldn't tell if it was me or Julie or Joanna. My confusion increased again when a third identical face appeared at my other shoulder and there were three of us in the mirror. I knew that one of them had to be me but for the life of me, I couldn't tell which it was.

The copy of Joanna in the middle was frowning in bewilderment while the other two smiled broadly and suddenly it all fit. The one in the middle was me, in my pink satin maid dress. Julie was, of course, in her green satin maid dress and Joanna was at my other shoulder. The face of the woman in the middle lit up in wonder. Now I knew who was who, I could see the slight differences, although at a glance anybody would have mistaken us for identical triplets or clones.

The three of us stared at each other in the mirror for a long moment, looking back and forth at each other in amazement. I had butterflies in my stomach and a rapidly growing erection in my panties caused by the heady mixture of seeing three identically beautiful women with the odd sensation caused by the notion that the reflection that didn't yet feel like my own was of a different woman and I was spying on her through her eyes.

Joanna and Julie both turned to congratulate and thank Susan. I couldn't tear my eyes away from the mirror; it didn't really feel like I was looking at a reflection, more that I was looking at a beautiful woman through a window or through someone else's eyes, seeing Joanna or Julie in the mirror instead of myself. It was a strangely intimate experience.

I was still in a half daze, both from the effects of the pill and the sight of my new reflection as Julie and I continued with our chores. Feeling light-headed as I was, I was even more grateful for her stern supervision. We served drinks and light snacks to Mistress Joanna and her guests and I felt even more elated at how pleased Mistress Joanna seemed with my conduct today.

Julie and I stood obediently next to each other as we awaited further instructions. I could feel the skirt and petticoats of her soft satin maid dress brushing against mine as we stood there and I gazed at her lovingly until she nudged me with her elbow and nodded her head towards Dr Carol.

"Come over here, girl," she ordered. "Yes Miss," I curtseyed and went to stand in front of her.

"It really is a very simple procedure," she was obviously continuing a conversation with Mistress Joanna that I hadn't been listening to. Dr Carol lifted the skirt of my dress. I blushed because I was still a little hard in my panties from being so close to Miss Julie but I knew MIstress Joanna would be angry if I disobeyed her guest.

"In fact," she continued, "it's even called a simple orchiectomy." She brushed the front of my panties, making me shiver at her touch on my erection. "Obviously she would look a lot better without this here but you would get some improvement," her hand moved between my legs to cup me through the satin, "by emptying these out. They'd be flatter in her panties and look a lot prettier." She looked up at me, still touching me through the satin, "You'd like to look prettier in your panties, wouldn't you, girl?"

With her hand where it was, I couldn't really curtsey but I touched the hem of my dress, bobbed my head slightly and replied, "Yes Miss, of course I would, if it would please Mistress Joanna and Miss Julie."

"See? She *wants* it done. I could do it now. Really, it would take me about half an hour then you'd never have to worry about her nasty male hormones ever again."

Mistress Joanna laughed, "You sound even more excited by the idea than Julie did earlier."

Dr Carol stroked me through my panties, making me gasp in pleasure. "It's just so…satisfying…to do that to a naughty little boy." I was getting even harder as she stroked me. "Knowing that once that step is taken by whoever owns him, the loss of his little willy surely won't be far behind." She pushed my skirt up even further. "I mean look at it. Disgusting."

I didn't know what boy she was talking about but surely boys didn't get their willies cut off. Only girls had to have their willies cut off. Wait…was that right?

"I totally agree," grimaced Joanna, "but it will be dealt with when I'm ready. I want to wean her off the pills and make sure the conditioning is sticking. Then I'll think about it."

I heard Miss Julie start to say something then immediately fall silent at a stern glance from Mistress Joanna.

"Thank you, Jenny," said Mistress Joanna, gesturing for me to go back to stand with Julie. Dr Carol dropped the front of my dress and I made a quick curtsey before going to stand with Julie, still aroused and flustered and a little confused by all the conversation.

Soon, Julie and I were dispatched to fetch Susan and Dr Carol's coats for them to leave. We both curtseyed and stood obediently waiting while Mistress Joanna bade them goodbye. After that we returned to our chores. I hadn't been given another pink pill so I found it a little easier to concentrate on what I was supposed to be doing and Mistress Julie hardly had to give me any spanks at all. The only times she did were when she caught me staring at my new reflection in wonder instead of doing what she had ordered.

When it was time for bed, we followed Mistress Joanna to the bedroom and undressed her, with lots of kisses and caresses. She stood there gloriously naked in front of us, stretching and yawning and I was hard in my panties just looking at her. My knees weakened at her smile and she stepped close to me, her hand gently touching my cheek and making me shiver with pleasure.

"You look so beautiful now, Jenny."

"Thank you Mistress Joanna," I curtseyed.

Her hand slipped round to the back of my neck and pulled my head close for a long, tender kiss as her other hand went round my waist. My lips were a little tender from whatever Susan had done to them earlier but it was worth it for the kiss as I melted into her arms and her tongue pushed its way into my mouth.

"You were perfect today," she whispered as she ended the kiss.

"Thank you Mistress Joanna," I gasped. "I was trying my best to be a good girl."

"You *are* a good girl, my dear. And I will make you an even better girl."

She let go of me and I staggered, knees still weak from the kiss.

"Kneel down for me, Jenny."

I curtseyed and obeyed.

"Good girl." She turned to Julie but still sounding like she was talking to me, "Julie, however, has been a naughty girl." Julie blanched and Joanna continued, "Arguing with me while I was having a discussion with Dr Carol, begging me for things I had already said no to."

"Sorry Mistress Joanna," said Julie with a curtsey. "I was just so excited at the thought of what Dr Carol wanted to do to her."

"So was I," replied Mistress Joanna, "but I managed to restrain myself. You've been a naughty girl and you don't have Jenny's poor performance as a maid to excuse you today. I think you need to be punished. Don't you think she needs to be punished, Jenny?"

I looked up at her, not sure what to say and stumbling over my words, "I...she...If you think she should, Mistress. She wasn't naughty on purpose."

"Hmmm. Perhaps I could excuse it if it was only once but she repeated her error. No, I think she definitely needs to be spanked." She turned back to me, "Would you like to spank her, Jenny? She enjoyed spanking you yesterday."

I felt tears well up in my eyes. I didn't want to punish Miss Julie! I wasn't even sure I would be able to bring myself to do it if Mistress Joanna ordered me to. I'd probably accept being spanked myself instead.

"Please don't make me do that, Mistress Joanna. She should be spanked if you think it is necessary but please don't make me do it. I...I can't."

Joanna smiled, "I think it might be fun watching you try one day. But not tonight, as you've been such a good girl."

She turned back to Julie and made a twirling gesture with her finger, "Turn round, Julie."

Julie curtseyed and obeyed and Mistress Joanna tied her hands behind her back with the bow of her apron. Joanna sat on the edge of the bed and pulled Julie over her lap, lifting her dress and tugging her panties down to expose her bottom. I knelt there, unable to tear my gaze away as Mistress Joanna delivered several hard spanks to Julie's bottom. Julie lay passively over her lap, wincing then apologising with each spank. Once again, I found myself inexplicably aroused by the sight of Mistress Joanna spanking her double, despite feeling bad for Julie getting punished. I still wasn't quite sure why she was being punished but I knew it was something to do with the discussions about me and this mystery boy Dr Carol was talking about earlier so I couldn't help feeling a little responsible even though Mistress Joanna had said it wasn't my fault.

Mistress Joanna was breathing heavily in arousal and her nipples were rock hard as she allowed Julie to slide off her lap to kneel on the floor before her, dress in array and panties still down around her thighs. Joanna's eyes were twinkling she stood and ran her fingers through her hair. "That's better."

She looked over at me. "Now, perhaps Jenny needs a little reward for being such a good girl today." She gestured for me to stand then made the same twirling gesture that she had made to Julie. Nervously I curtseyed and turned round, wondering if she was also going to spank me for something. She grabbed my wrists and tied them behind my back with my apron ribbons. She turned me back round and sat at her dresser, gesturing for me to come and stand next to her.

I gasped and leaned back against the dresser for support as she ran one long fingernail, slowly up my smooth leg and under the petticoats of my dress. I closed my eyes and moaned softly as her hand found my erection and began to stroke me through my satin panties.

"Does that feel nice, Jenny?"

"Yes Mistress!" I managed to gasp, "Thank you Mistress Joanna!"

"Don't get too used to it; it won't always be there."

I gasped in frustration as her hand moved down to caress my thigh. I opened my eye to see her summoning Julie, who struggled to her feet with her hands still tied. Joanna, stunning in her nakedness, opened her legs and gestured for Julie to kneel. Julie carefully knelt then leant her head forward to kiss and lick between Mistress Joanna's legs. I gasped at the sight and Mistress Joanna rolled her head back, her breathing becoming heavy again and her nipples stiffening once more. Her hand moved back onto my erection.

"This is your last chance to be a good girl tonight, Julie. If Jenny comes before I do, no fun for you."

I heard Julie moan in frustration and Mistress Joanna gasped, her hand jumping against my erection as Julie redoubled her efforts between her legs.

With my hands tied and the overwhelming pleasure of Mistress Joanna's touch, there was nothing I could do but lean back against the dresser and let her do whatever she wanted to me.

The three of us gasped and moaned in unison and I could feel an orgasm approaching. I was desperate for Mistress Joanna to keep touching me, to make me come but also desperate for her to come first so that Julie would also be touched by her. I began to squirm, wriggling in pleasure and desperation not to come yet but utterly unable to do anything to stop it. With a final gasp and a long moan, I came, spurting in my panties as Mistress Joanna rubbed me. I heard Julie gasping, frantically trying to make Mistress Joanna come but it was too late.

I collapsed weakly against the dresser, shuddering at each movement of Joanna's hand and each twitch of my erection as the orgasm subsided. I leant there, drained and gulping for breath as Mistress Joanna removed her hand from under my dress and grabbed Julie's head, holding her tightly between her legs as Julie continued to lick her. All I could do was lean there staring at the enraptured look on her face as Julie finally brought her to orgasm.

When she'd recovered slightly, Mistress Joanna stood and untied my hands. "Help me into my nightie, Jenny."

"Yes Mistress Joanna," I replied with a wobbly curtsey. I selected an ankle length black satin nightie and slipped it over her head. "Mmmm!" she sighed as she ran her hands down over her sides, smoothing the sexy material down over her even sexier body.

"You may stand now, Julie," she said as she draped herself on the bed, watching us. Julie climbed to her feet, hands still tied and stood next to me. I could see she was aroused as her nipples were visible even through her bra and dress.

"You were too slow, Julie dear. No fun for you tonight, I'm afraid. But perhaps she deserves a little consolation kiss, eh Jenny?"

"Yes Mistress Joanna."

"Go on then."

"Yes Mistress," I curtseyed. I slid my arms around Julie's neck and gave her a tender, loving kiss, then another. Her head moved forward and she kissed me hungrily, her tongue forcing its way into my mouth. She pressed her groin against mine but I'd already orgasmed and my erection was shrinking rapidly. Between that and two layers of petticoats and skirts, there was nothing for her to press against and I heard her moan in frustration, kissing me even more roughly. Mistress Joanna was sighing happily, running her hands up and down her body through the satin nightie as she watched her doubles kissing.

She stretched and yawned. "I'm sleepy. Get into your nighties, girls."

Miss Julie gave another frustrated gasp as I ended the kiss and walked behind her to untie her hands. We unzipped each other's dresses and Julie helped me wipe myself clean when I removed my panties. We put on nighties that matched Mistress Joanna's – in our own colours of course.

We were just about to climb into bed when Mistress Joanna said sleepily, "Jenny – look in that drawer there. Find Julie's collar. I haven't had to use it for ages but I think she needs it to make sure she behaves herself tonight and doesn't do anything naughty like touching herself while we're asleep."

"Yes Mistress." I found the collar – a match in green satin for the one they'd made me wear yesterday. "Sorry," I whispered to Julie as she allowed me to fasten it round her neck and tie the ribbons round her wrists.

"That's better," smiled Mistress Joanna as she looked to make sure that Julie wouldn't be able to reach between her legs in the night.

We climbed into bed and the three of us snuggled together, bodies pressing close in our soft satin nighties. Mistress Joanna was asleep almost instantly but Julie was obviously still very frustrated as she fidgeted and kept me awake for a while.

Six

I don't know how long they kept me at the house. It might have only been the two weeks they originally mentioned or it might have been months. I began to forget anything about the world or my life before I'd come to the house. Somewhere inside I knew that it wasn't my reflection I was seeing in the mirror each day. It looked like Mistress Joanna and Miss Julie but it was obviously me. Even without makeup I looked like Joanna and Julie – I had a very similar mouth now and my eyebrows matched theirs in shape and colour and whatever Susan had done to my eyes remained, the dark liner and tinted lashes making me look even more like them. The strange disorientation of that gradually went away and I was thrilled to see that beautiful face in the mirror - what more beautiful sight could there be?

I had no idea what face I should have been seeing in the mirror. I couldn't picture anything else that might be there or recall ever seeing a different face. Had I always looked like them? Every now and then, something seemed a little...off...about being called a girl but I couldn't put my finger on it. What else was there? I knew I had a willy but I couldn't always remember if it was meant to be there. I couldn't even always remember for sure if Mistress Joanna or Miss Julie had a willy, until I saw them naked of course. I sometimes even forgot that it was there at all – Mistress Joanna only ever touched it through my nightie or panties and Miss Julie generally only got to use it while Mistress Joanna was straddling me, using my mouth for her pleasure.

Most of the time, it just embarrassed me when it got hard and reminded me that I wasn't as perfect as Mistress Joanna and the embarrassment was only made worse by how good it felt for it to be touched. I even jumped once when I caught a glimpse of it as I showered, forgetting it was there and being surprised to see it. It only took me an instant to remember what it was but I was trembling with shock for minutes afterwards – the same way anyone would react to suddenly finding a lump on their body that wasn't supposed to be there.

Because Mistress Joanna was pleased, I was also pleased when she pointed out that my corset was becoming a little less tight and the cups a little less loose. I guess all the massage was working. I had to ask them to be a little more gentle when massaging my chest as it was tender at times but gentle massage of my chest felt amazing, like scratching an itch deep inside but even better. The soft satin of my corset always felt cool and comforting against my chest and nipples after a massage.

Gradually, being given the little pink pills became less and less frequent. I didn't really notice any difference and vaguely wondered why I'd been taking them in the first place. Perhaps they hadn't worked properly and that was why I didn't have to take one so often.

I also got better at my maid duties, hardly ever needing to be spanked. Sometimes Mistress Joanna liked to spank me anyway, even though I wasn't sure I had done anything wrong. But she seemed certain that I deserved it so she must have been right. Those times made me feel bad though, as I struggled to work out what I'd done wrong to make sure that I didn't do it again. I felt even worse the times she spanked Miss Julie for something I'd done. I sometimes wondered if I'd always been a maid but that was another thing I couldn't recall ever being different before coming to their house. It felt like I'd always been here.

There were occasional visits from Dr Carol, who took more of my blood or gave me injections. I didn't really know what they were for and was too embarrassed to admit that I didn't really understand the technical explanations she gave as she injected me. I did manage to fathom that she was helping me to be a good girl and to be more perfect for Mistress Joanna so I happily let her get on with her job.

One afternoon while she was there, Julie and I were serving drinks to Dr Carol and Mistress Joanna in the living room. As I crouched to put Dr Carol's drink on the coffee table, my knee trembled and I had to put my hand out to steady myself. I put the cup and saucer down heavily and tea sploshed from the cup into the saucer.

Dr Carol sighed angrily, "You stupid girl!"

I got to my feet, apologising. "Sorry Miss, I'll get a cloth." I curtseyed and hurried from the room to fetch a cloth and a clean saucer. I dried the bottom of her cup and put it in the new saucer and wiped the tea from the wet saucer. "Sorry," I curtseyed again.

"You've embarrassed me in front of my guest," frowned Mistress Joanna.

Tears were starting as I curtseyed again, "I'm sorry Mistress. It was an accident. I won't do it again."

"No, this is unacceptable. I was undecided earlier today but now you've made my decision for me. You've come far enough as a girl now. I'm going to let Dr Carol perform the procedure she has been suggesting."

I looked in confusion, wondering what she was talking about. I heard Julie clap her hands behind me in glee, "Yay!"

Joanna glared at her. "That's enough from you, Julie. You're senior maid, I also hold you responsible for Jenny's mistakes."

Julie looked contrite and curtseyed, "Sorry Mistress Joanna."

"Do you have the necessary equipment with you Carol?"

"Always!" beamed Dr Carol, looking excited.

"Then it's decided."

Julie was looking even more excited than Dr Carol but kept her mouth shut. Joanna approached me and stroked my cheek gently, "Dr Carol is going to make you even more perfect for me. You'd like that, wouldn't you Jenny?"

I curtseyed again, starting to get hard in my panties at the look on her face, the caress of her hand on my face and thought of being able to please her to make up for my mistake. "Yes Mistress Joanna," I breathed. "I want to be a good girl and be even more perfect for you."

"You will be." Her hand moved down from my face to caress me through the front of my satin dress and the cups of my corset. I could feel my nipples stiffen under her hand as my erection continued to grow. Mistress Joanna looked aroused too, I could see her nipples harden through the thin blouse, which only made my erection get even harder.

"Then Dr Carol can perform her procedure."

"Thank you Dr Carol," I said, surprised to see that she too looked aroused and wondering what was going on.

Joanna kept her hand on my chest, touching me through my soft satin as she turned her head towards Julie. "But Julie needs punishing too, so why stop there?"

"Wait Mistress…" began Julie but Joanna continued.

"I think it might be time for the full thing."

Julie gasped, looking about to protest and I begged her with my eyes not to anger Mistress Joanna, I didn't want to see Julie punished.

"You know I can't do a full vaginoplasty," said Dr Carol.

"I know. You can do your thing today but I can start arranging the rest."

"Please Mistress…I…" Julie looked scared and I willed her to stop talking. Why was she making Mistress Joanna angry at her? Why couldn't she just let Mistress Joanna punish me instead of being punished for my mistake too?

Joanna grinned wickedly. "I've got a fun idea. Jenny here has blubbed whenever I've suggested that she should be the one who spanks Julie. But I think I'd like to see that. She should be given a chance to please me. You want to please me, don't you Jenny?"

"Yes Mistress." I didn't want to spank Julie but if she carried on angering Mistress Joanna then being spanked by me was probably less of a punishment than whatever Mistress Joanna had in mind.

"Good girl. So Julie…Jenny is going to try to spank you and I want you to try to spank her. The winner is whoever manages to tie the other girl's hands behind her back with her apron ribbons. If Julie wins, then Jenny's punishment is a spanking from Julie before her orchiectomy…but if Jenny wins, Julie's punishment is a spanking from Jenny before I arrange the vaginoplasty."

Julie gasped. I still wasn't sure what some of the words meant but I could see that Julie was shocked by the idea of being spanked by me. I knew that I would have to try my hardest to do so though. As much as I hated the idea of having to spank her, it was clear that if I managed to do it then Mistress Joanna would be pleased, Julie would avoid further punishment on my behalf and then Dr Carol would be allowed to do whatever it was she was going to do to make me prettier and make Mistress Joanna happy. Whatever it was would obviously also make Dr Carol and Miss Julie happy too, so that was even more reason to try my hardest to be a good girl for Mistress Joanna and give Julie her spanking.

Mistress Joanna took us up to the exercise room while Dr Carol fetched something from her car. As we waited for Dr Carol to return, Julie whispered to me, "You have to let me win. Don't fight me, just let me tie you up and spank you. I promise not to spank you as hard as usual."

I shook my head, "No. I have to be a good girl and try to win, to please Mistress Joanna. If I don't then she might not let Dr Carol make me prettier."

Julie looked desperate, "You don't understand. If you win, Joanna is going to have your willy cut off."

I frowned, "She didn't say that. She didn't say anything about Dr Carol cutting my willy off. That's not a thing that happens, is it?"

"No, not Dr Carol. She's going to do an orchiectomy."

There was that word again, I had no idea what it meant and that must have shown on my face because Julie continued with a sigh, "That means she's going to empty out your balls."

I didn't have the faintest idea what that could possibly mean. Who on earth used balls as containers? I tried to imagine what someone might keep in balls that would need emptying. I struggled to catch up with the conversation, "But she won't do that if I win?"

Julie was looking exasperated as well now, "Yes of course she's going to do that if you win!"

I smiled, "Then I need to try to win, don't I?" I felt sorry for her – she was obviously as confused by all this as I was. "If that's what's going to make me prettier. You want me to be prettier don't you?"

"Yes of course but she's going to do that either way. You need to let me win or Joanna will do even more."

"Why don't you want me to be prettier?"

"I do! Just not like that. Trust me, you don't want it like that either. She's going to cut your willy off if you win, that's what she meant by vagi…"

"Now, now girls, no talking," ordered Mistress Joanna sternly. We both curtseyed and stood in silence for a few moments until Dr Carol reappeared carrying a medium sized holdall.

Mistress Joanna gestured for us to step onto the matted area of the exercise room. It was about fifteen feet square. "Let me win!" hissed Julie quietly as we walked onto the mats and stood a few feet apart, facing each other. I shook my head, why couldn't she understand? I had to beat her then she'd see that I was right.

"Now, no kicking or biting, girls and if one of you gets knocked off the mats, you lose."

I wondered if she was going to tell us when to start but Julie rushed at me, trying to grab my arms. I squeaked and danced out of her way. She darted forward and flicked up the front of my maid dress, taunting me. I moved away, circling round her and back towards the centre of the mats.

She lunged at my skirt again and I grabbed her arm with both hands. She tried to pull away but I held on tight with no real plan as to how to get the arm behind her back and tied with her apron ribbons. She stopped trying to pull away and instead pushed back at me, forcing me to stumble backwards towards the edge of the mat.

I tripped over my own feet and we went down, my legs tangling in hers. As we tumbled one of my hands lost grip on her arm but the other managed to hang on. We rolled and suddenly I was on top and Julie was lying on her side with one arm trapped beneath her.

We froze for an instant before both realising that I had the advantage. Julie cried out and started thrashing beneath me as I grabbed her arm with my other hand and tried to pull it behind her back. Mistress Joanna was cheering and clapping excitedly, "Go on, Jenny!"

As I wrestled with her, I couldn't believe how much she was thrashing about and how scared she sounded as she begged me to stop. I held onto her arm as tightly as I could, using all my weight to push it back behind her. "Let me tie you up!" I gasped. "You need to stop fighting me!" I was almost in tears in my desperation to beat her and save her from a worse punishment on my account but she wouldn't stop wriggling.

I'd almost got her hand to the loop in the bow of her apron ribbon and was trying to push it through when she managed to get a leg under her. "No no no no no!" she was screaming as I got the loop of satin ribbon over her fingertips. She pushed violently on the leg beneath her and bucked so hard that I lost my grip and was thrown off her, landing on my back and stunned for a second.

By the time I managed to start struggling to my feet, Jenny was standing and rushing towards me. I put my hands up to fend her off and she grabbed my wrists. Her momentum pushed me back down and she fell on top of me, still holding my wrists and pinning me to the mat with her body, her hands holding mine firmly to the floor above my head. I wriggled beneath her helplessly and she paused for a moment, getting her breath back and working out what to do next.

She leaned forward and kissed me. I froze and she kissed me again. In surprise, I stopped struggling and began to respond to her kiss. She was moaning sexily now as she kissed me and I began to get hard in my panties. Her kisses became more passionate, her tongue forcing its way into my mouth as I lay there, pinned and completely unable to resist. I could hear Mistress Joanna laughing excitedly at the sight.

We kissed for a long moment, the fight forgotten as our passion became more urgent and I eagerly sought more kisses from the woman I loved. I was completely hard now. The skirts and petticoats of our maid dresses were rucked up against each other and I gasped as I felt her grind her groin against my erection.

Julie changed position, sitting up, still straddling me. Her hands kept tight grip on my wrists but the pulled them down, pinning my arms to the floor at my sides, rubbing herself against my satin-covered erection as I lay gasping and moaning beneath her. Lost in the throes of passion I could barely take my eyes off the beautiful woman above me, using me for her pleasure.

I heard another sexy moan and glanced over, seeing Mistress Joanna with her hand up her skirt between her legs, aroused by the sight of her two doubles. I moaned again, watching Mistress Joanna touch herself as Julie's thrusts against me became more urgent. I could barely move but I tried to wriggle my hips in time with her strokes against me. I closed my eyes, panting as I could feel the impending orgasm. Julie was gasping in time with my panting and her fingers dug harder into my wrists, pushing my hands under me, behind my back as I lay beneath her.

"Oh yes, oh yes, oh yes!" I was gasping as I felt the pressure rise and knew that I had passed the point of no return. "Ohhhhhhhhh!" I moaned as I started to spurt in my panties.

Immediately Julie swung one of her legs off me and rolled me onto my front, still in the throes of my orgasm. She grabbed my wrists and pulled them behind me, wrapping the ribbon of my apron quickly round them.

"No!" I cried as the last few spasms twitched in my panties. "Please don't do this!" I struggled weakly. One hand just about slipped free and I felt her grab for it but she let it go to keep hold of my other hand. I felt her push it through the loop of the ribbon and pull it tight, stopping me from pulling it out while she tied a knot to keep it there.

When she had that hand secure she grabbed for my free hand. I was too weak to do much to stop her and was begging her not to tie me up and to let me win. She pulled my hand behind my back and I did the only thing I could – roll with it. She was surprised when I moved towards her instead of trying to get away. I knocked her to the side and she had to let go of my arm to steady herself. I rolled away from her, struggling to get to my feet with one hand tied behind my back.

I felt drained – weak and shaky and had trouble standing. Julie was a lot quicker getting to her feet and coming back towards me. If I didn't do something quick, she would easily overpower me and tie my other hand. She was going to win and ruin everything! Why couldn't she understand that I needed to win? That letting me win was the best for all of us?

I was desperate. I knew I couldn't fight her off if she got her hands on me again. I was too weak and only had one free arm. I lunged forward, grabbing her round the waist with my free arm and throwing all my weight against her. She screamed in panic as she realised what I was doing – trying to push her off the mats.

"No! Don't!" she gasped as she staggered back a couple of paces then dropped, collapsing to the floor rather than get pushed back any further. We rolled again and I nearly slid off the edge of the mat. I was laying on my front and hurried to drag myself properly back onto the mats with my free arm but I was too slow. Julie scrabbled quickly towards me and threw her weight on top of me, pinning me face down on the mat as she grabbed my arm and pushed it behind me.

I struggled but I had no strength left and I began to sob as I begged her to stop what she was doing and let me go. It was all over within seconds. Julie pushed my other hand through the loop of my apron ribbon and pulled it tight. I stopped struggling and just lay there sobbing as Julie collapsed on top of me, panting with the exertion.

Mistress Joanna and Dr Carol were applauding.

Julie rolled off me and sat on the mat, legs outstretched. She hauled me over her lap and pushed the back of my dress and my petticoats up to expose my satin-clad bottom. Her spanks were a lot gentler than usual, more for show than punishment this time. I offered no resistance, just lay there sobbing, distraught that I had disobeyed Mistress Joanna, had probably caused Julie to be punished for my mistake and that Dr Carol might not be allowed to make me prettier for Joanna and Julie.

When she finished spanking me, Julie helped me to my feet and smoothed down my petticoats and dress. Then she hugged me, whispering in my ear, "That was too close, you silly girl. You almost lost your willy as well as your balls."

I sobbed on her shoulder as she held me, feeling comforted by her arms around me and her body pressed against mine through our satin dresses.

Mistress Joanna walked over to us and gave us both a hug. "That was wonderful, girls! I think we should do this again some time." Her face was flushed and her nipples were hard under her blouse. She was breathing heavily and looked exactly like she did whenever the two of us gave her an orgasm while dressing her in the morning.

"Well done, Julie. It looks like you get to keep your favourite plaything for a while longer."

Julie curtseyed with a huge smile on her face, "Thank you Mistress Joanna."

Dr Carol was also looking flushed and was fanning her face with her hand. "The things you get up to with your girls, Joanna!"

Mistress Joanna grinned at her, "Now it's time for you to have your fun, Carol."

Dr Carol grinned at me, "Time to make you prettier for your Mistress, Jenny my dear."

Julie was bouncing on her toes with excitement and I sniffed away a tear. "You mean I'm still allowed to be prettier for you, Mistress Joanna?"

"Of course, darling!"

I sighed with relief.

"Dr Carol will make you a little prettier now and next time we do this, if you manage to win and tie Julie up, then I'll arrange to make you perfect!"

My distress forgotten, I thanked her profusely. I still hadn't quite worked out what Dr Carol was going to do to me but I was ecstatic that I hadn't angered Mistress Joanna any more. The two women seemed to have forgiven me for spilling the tea and now Dr Carol was going to make me prettier for Mistress Joanna even though I hadn't managed to tie Julie up!

"Let's get you over to the table, dear," said Dr Carol, picking up her holdall. I followed her to the massage table where Julie untied my hands long enough for me to lie on the table and for her to tie my hands to the bar above my head. Julie pushed the hem of my dress and my petticoats up and tugged my panties off to wipe me clean while Dr Carol injected something into my arm. "Just a little sedative, Jenny. It's to keep you calm while I perform the procedure. It will help you sleep afterwards too."

"Thank you Dr Carol," I smiled.

Dr Carol fastened my ankles into the stirrups at the bottom of the table and spread my legs wide apart. It didn't take long for the sedative to start working. I began to feel pleasantly sleepy and my eyes half closed. I felt a little like I was wrapped in cotton wool.

Julie stood to the side, watching excitedly and Mistress Joanna stood with her hand draped over Julie's shoulder, breathing heavily and looking gorgeously sexy as she listened to Dr Carol explain what she was doing.

"I'll be using a local anaesthetic. No need for a general for a simple procedure like this. And some of the ladies I do this for like their girls to be awake and aware of exactly what is happening to them."

I felt something wet touch me between my legs. I gasped and bit my lip at a sudden pricking sensation, similar to the injection she'd given me in my arm.

"This should work pretty quickly."

I felt a growing coldness between my legs. It swiftly became intensely chilly but not unpleasant. It faded after a short while then nothing. There was no feeling between my legs at all.

"See? I can pinch or squeeze them and she doesn't feel a thing."

I was vaguely aware that she was doing something between my legs but I couldn't really *feel* it. I looked down but with my dress and petticoats rucked up round my waist, I couldn't see past them or see anything Dr Carol was doing. I wondered again what she could be doing to make me prettier but I was feeling too sleepy to worry about it much. Whatever she was doing didn't seem to be painful at all and from the looks on Mistress Joanna's and Miss Julie's faces, they were very excited to see it happening. I'm sure I'd be able to see what she did when she'd finished.

"So now we make a small incision here," said Dr Carol.

I lay there half-asleep, smiling happily at Mistress Joanna and Miss Julie as Dr Carol did whatever it was she was doing.

"This is the tricky bit, carefully pulling them out through the incision."

I was aware of a vague tugging between my legs but still couldn't really feel anything, as if it were happening to someone else and I'd just been told about it.

I closed my eyes and must have dozed off for a while because when I opened them again Dr Carol was saying, "That's it, here comes the other one." I was aware of the vague tugging again. I still couldn't feel anything but there was an odd sensation of emptiness somewhere in the pit of my stomach. A bit like when you get butterflies.

I looked down but my dress was still in the way.

"Last chance to change your mind?" said Dr Carol.

"Do it!" breathed Mistress Joanna, sexily.

"A quick cut here...and done!"

I looked over at Mistress Joanna and Miss Julie. Dr Carol was holding a small dish out to show them something. Mistress Joanna was looking very aroused now, her hand over Julie's shoulder and caressing her nipple through her maid dress. Her other hand was under her skirt again. Miss Julie was also looking excited but with a sort of fascinated grimace on her face.

Dr Carol put the dish down. "Too late to change your mind now, Joanna. This is permanent. No going back and no more testosterone for this girly, ever."

Both Joanna and Julie gasped in excitement and I smiled, glad to see them both so happy.

"I didn't bring any prosthetics with me," said Dr Carol. "I assumed you didn't want them."

"Absolutely not," agreed Mistress Joanna.

"Then a couple of stitches and a dressing and we're finished." She went back to work between my legs. When she'd finished what she was doing, Joanna and Julie stepped round between my legs to inspect her work. I could see them both reaching out to touch me between my legs. I still couldn't feel anything and whimpered quietly at the frustration of not being able to feel Mistress Joanna touching me there.

"It's so much prettier!" enthused Mistress Joanna.

"Oh yes!" breathed Miss Julie. I saw them reaching to touch me again but still nothing.

"Oh!" gasped Julie. "It moved. Is it trying to get hard?"

Dr Carol laughed, "Don't worry, it's only the anaesthetic stopping it. There's nothing stopping her getting hard when she comes out of it."

"While she's still got it, at least," added Mistress Joanna, grinning at the pout on Julie's face as she said it.

"I'll just put a dressing on it," said Dr Carol, going back to work between my legs. "It will take a few days to heal. Be gentle with her and try to stop her touching it for a couple of days at least. You don't need to give her any more anti-androgens. Keep the doses of the other hormones at the same level. I'll monitor them but you can expect them to have an increased effect from now on."

I lay there enjoying the happy looks on the faces of Joanna and Julie while Dr Carol finished.

Mistress Joanna thanked her profusely as she repacked her holdall and I managed a sleepy, "Thank you Dr Carol."

Mistress Joanna went to see her out while Miss Julie untied me from the massage table and helped me climb down. She rearranged my skirt and petticoats and led me through to the bedroom. I was incredibly sleepy and walking strangely because of the anaesthetic making it feel like there was nothing at all where my groin should be. It reminded me of when you go to the dentist and afterwards you can't feel the side of your face, like it's not there even though you know your tongue is pressing against it. Like that but a lot stranger.

I was nearly asleep on my feet as Miss Julie helped me out of my maid dress and corset and slipped a long pink satin nightie onto me. Mistress Joanna came back in and said, "Don't forget her collar."

I tried to recall why she wanted my collar and ended up sobbing, begging her not to make me wear it and apologising, promising to be a god girl.

"Shhh," she comforted me. "I'm not punishing you. You're a good girl and I'm very proud of you. This is for your own good, to protect you because you've been such a good girl and let Dr Carol make you prettier for me."

I wiped a tear away and let Julie put the collar on me and tie the ribbons round my wrists. Julie helped me into bed before undressing Mistress Joanna and herself then putting matching nighties on both of them.

I smiled happily as I watched Mistress Joanna start to kiss Julie, caressing her through her dark green satin nightie, making her gasp as she tweaked one of Julie's hard nipples. She led Julie to the bed and they lay down next to me. Mistress Joanna reached out a hand and started to caress one of the two fleshy, sensitive bumps on my chest through my satin nightie as Julie kissed her way down Joanna's body then pushed the hem of her nightie up and lowered her head between Mistress Joanna's legs.

I sighed happily as Mistress Joanna caressed me, my small nipple growing hard under her fingers, but I was asleep within seconds.

Seven

Mistress Joanna kept me in bed most of the time for the next couple of days. I was still wearing my collar so I couldn't touch between my legs or feel what Dr Carol had been up to down there. It was a little sore if I moved suddenly but was okay most of the time. It itched a little occasionally and when Mistress Joanna caught me trying – futilely – to reach to scratch she allowed Miss Julie, in one of her beautiful green satin maid dresses, to gently stroke me between my legs to soothe me.

I lay there, eyes closed and moaning in pleasure as she tenderly stroked me through my satin nightie with her long fingernails. I saw her smile as she watched me getting hard under the nightie and her other hand began to stroke my erection through it.

"Dr Carol was right! It does still work!" she grinned at Mistress Joanna.

"That's a shame," replied Mistress Joanna.

I lay there, unable to do anything but let Miss Julie touch me. I was gasping and moaning under her hands and could feel my orgasm approaching. Suddenly my erection was twitching under the nightie as the orgasm hit me and I spurted into the satin.

Julie continued touching me gently as I recovered then helped me off the bed to get into a clean nightie. She had to untie my wrists from the ribbons so I could take the nightie off.

"You've hardly made a mess of it at all!" she said in wonder. "Virtually nothing came out." She giggled, "I should have realised that would happen."

I stood there naked as she selected another nightie for me. I looked in the mirror but couldn't really see anything different about myself. With my hands free, I reached between my legs. My willy was still there, obviously, but there was a sort of flap of skin under it. I was pretty sure that hadn't been there before and I was very confused by it. I knew that hadn't always been there but how was it possible for it to feel like something new was there but also that something was missing? What had Dr Carol done to make me prettier? Whatever it was didn't feel like anything that Joanna or Julie had between their legs.

"Stop that," said Mistress Joanna, looking up and seeing me touching between my legs.

"Sorry Mistress Joanna," I curtseyed.

Julie helped me into a beautiful short pink satin babydoll nightie with matching panties then tied my wrists with the ribbons again and I forgot my confusion as they took me downstairs so I could sit with Mistress Joanna while Julie prepared lunch.

After a couple of days I was back in my maid dress, helping Julie as usual and happy to be out of bed and looking after Mistress Joanna.

Some days later, Mistress Joanna announced that we were going out for lunch. Julie clapped her hands in excitement and smiled happily at me. "Your first outing as one of us! You'd better be on your best behaviour."

"Yes Miss Julie," I curtseyed. As we started to get ready I began to feel nervous. I couldn't really remember anything about my time before coming to this house. I had vague memories of being out before and I was pretty sure that Joanna and Julie had a house in town somewhere that I had spent a lot of time at. The nervousness started to become more like fear and I didn't understand it. Going out for lunch shouldn't be such a big thing, should it?

As we put on our matching bras and panties and did our makeup I wondered why getting ready to go out didn't feel more familiar, like something normal. I checked my lipstick and my hair in the mirror – everything looked perfect and I was just as pretty as Miss Julie or Mistress Joanna, so why was I still feeling so shaky and out of place as I fastened the buttons of my beautiful hot pink satin blouse and tucked it into the short black satin skirt? I was about to go out and enjoy myself with the two most beautiful women in the world – Joanna in her black satin blouse and Julie in her emerald green satin blouse, all three of us wearing identical skirts and makeup. What could be more normal than this?

I was certain that I had been out for lunch with these two women several times before, so why did it feel like this was the first time?

Was it something about my skirt? It was a little short but not indecently so. Perhaps I usually wore a longer skirt? I had a brief flash of something else, a different sort of item of clothing to wear on my lower half but it was gone almost instantly. I found that I couldn't remember what I had been wearing any of the other times I'd been out somewhere with them. It all seemed so long ago and the vague memories were confusing, seeming as if they were someone else's, someone who looked nothing like me or the two women.

As I slipped the low-heeled pink suede court shoes onto my feet and Julie handed me a pink satin clutch bag, I wondered if it was the shoes. I usually wore canvas pumps with my maid dresses. These shoes felt strange. Not uncomfortable but just odd, as if I'd never worn heels before. They were only about an inch but I felt stilted and odd taking a few steps in them. Surely I must have worn heels before? How could a girl get to my age without ever having worn heels? But this odd feeling had been coming on long before I put the shoes on so it couldn't be that.

My nervousness increased as Julie threw a pink scarf artfully round my shoulders and, with a final check of our appearance in the mirror, Mistress Joanna led us downstairs and to the front door. I couldn't remember stepping through this door and I was trembling as she opened it. Julie hooked her arm in mine and gave me a kiss on the cheek. "You look beautiful, Jenny. No need to be nervous, we're just three girls going out for lunch. Relax and enjoy yourself."

As we stepped outside to see a car and a driver waiting for us, I felt like running back inside. I still couldn't understand why I was having this reaction and clung tightly to Julie as the driver held the door for us. Joanna slipped into the plush leather seating inside and I tried to copy how she had done so, smoothing my skirt down, sitting and swinging my legs into the car, to sit facing her. I slid across the seat and Julie sat next to me, holding my hand.

"Don't look so scared," said Joanna.

"I'm sorry Mistress Joanna," I replied. "I don't know why I feel so nervous all of a sudden."

Joanna and Julie shared a look. "I wish he could remember more," whispered Julie to Joanna. "It would be such a turn on to hear him begging us not to make him go out as a girl!"

They both laughed and I looked on in confusion, wondering who they were talking about. I glanced at the driver who was climbing into the driving seat. They weren't talking about him were they? My mouth popped open in astonishment – the driver wasn't a girl! He was a…a boy? No, a man. I tried to remember what was significant about that; it suddenly felt really important that I remember…something. Something about how boys and girls are different? Something about…? I struggled to think clearly. There was definitely something important…what was it? Something only boys had…a willy? No that couldn't be right, could it? I had a willy and I was a girl. But the other women didn't have them.

Somewhere in the back of my mind, I knew that Joanna was turning me into a copy of her – and that was a wonderful thing! – but what had I been before? Suddenly the clothing I was wearing felt completely alien to me. The slippery satin skirt that clung tightly round my thighs felt strange. It really didn't feel like I had worn something like this before. What else could I have worn? Trousers! Like the driver was wearing! Did I used to wear trousers? I couldn't really remember and that certainly didn't seem right.

I glanced down at the front of my blouse where the padded cups of my bra pressed the material out. I knew I was smaller there than Joanna or Julie, that's why my bra was so padded. It felt comfortable to be wearing it, feeling it nestling my small breasts inside the soft satin but why did it seem such a strange thing? Boys didn't have breasts, did they? I still couldn't remember for sure.

Was I a boy or a girl? Being a girl didn't seem right. I was *becoming* a girl, wasn't I? I was being turned into one to please Mistress Joanna. But the thought of being a boy seemed ridiculous. Was I just becoming more of a girl? That must be it. But what had Dr Carol done to me? Boys had something else between their legs, didn't they? Did I? I was pretty sure that boys didn't just have a strange flap of skin there but I was also pretty sure that girls didn't either. I couldn't quite remember what boys *did* have there and tried to work out if Dr Carol had taken something away from me.

The car pulled off and Julie squeezed my hand and started talking to me in her hypnotic way, blowing all other thoughts out of my head. She was telling me how pretty I was, how much I loved being a girl like them, how much I wanted to be a good girl for Mistress Joanna – on and on as the car drove through several miles of countryside.

The nervousness was easing and I wondered why it had seemed such a big thing. Even if this was the first time I'd gone out for lunch with them, it shouldn't feel this strange. Not wrong exactly, more like there had been some sort of mistake about something. I was just nervous about pleasing Mistress Joanna by being her double along with Julie. That must be it. Perhaps it felt odd because previously I would have worn a different sort of skirt or something. All I had to do was concentrate on being a good girl for Mistress Joanna and surely everything would be okay.

I settled back into the plush leather seat, happily listening to Julie's words without really taking them in and smiling contentedly at Mistress Joanna; hard in my knickers and enjoying the tingling in my breasts as the motion of the car caused my nipples to move against the soft satin cups of my bra. My nipples seemed to have been feeling a lot more sensitive recently and the slightest touch of them through my nightie from Joanna or Julie made me moan with pleasure. Even the feeling of them brushing against my maid dress made me hard in my panties at all sorts of random times.

I was half asleep, in a trance as the car pulled up somewhere and Julie said, "We're here, Jenny."

The driver held the door for us to step out of the car. I felt some of the nervousness return as I stood next to Joanna and Julie, smoothing my skirt down and adjusting the scarf round my shoulders. Nothing about this seemed familiar. Joanna stepped towards the restaurant door with Julie and me a step behind her. Someone opened the door for her and we walked into an incredibly posh restaurant. The head waiter was greeting us enthusiastically. He obviously knew who Joanna was and seemed pleasantly surprised when I was introduced as Jenny, Joanna's other sister.

Heads turned as we were led to our seats and a waiter held each of our chairs for us to sit. I wasn't used to this sort of attention –

virtually everyone in the restaurant was looking over at us. I felt a little nervous but I was pretty sure that I had never been in such an expensive-looking restaurant before, so that was probably why this didn't feel like something I had done before. It was also new to me to realise that people were staring, seeing three gorgeous redheaded triplets. The looks one of the men was giving us creeped me out a little so I tried to avoid eye contact with the other diners, wanting only to drink in the beauty of the two women I was lucky enough to be with and be one of.

The food was exquisite. We dined slowly, with Mistress Joanna doing most of the talking. I tried to join in the conversation where I could but, as usual, my thoughts got a little fuzzy when I tried to think of anything but Joanna and Julie.

Heads turned again as we got up to leave. I blushed as the head waiter told us what a pleasure it had been to serve three such beautiful ladies. I wasn't sure I liked it very much and it made me feel a little uneasy that I couldn't recall being in such a situation before. Had I been a very plain girl before meeting Mistress Joanna? I knew that, really, he was complimenting Joanna. Julie and I just happened to look a lot like her now and I tried to cling to that thought – that she had made me prettier and beautiful like her and just wanted me to be perfect and a good girl for her.

The driver was waiting for us outside with the car and we climbed in. He drove us somewhere else and soon we found ourselves in a very exclusive clothing boutique where Mistress Joanna was again greeted as an old friend. I too was greeted warmly when introduced as her sister. We spent an hour or so in the boutique with Julie and me trying on a variety of dresses while Mistress Joanna relaxed with a glass of wine and watched us model them.

Despite this also feeling like something entirely new to me, I found myself enjoying the time there, Julie and I helping each other into and out of our dresses and posing in them for Mistress Joanna to admire. It just made me happy to be standing there while Mistress Joanna inspected me and smiled.

She chose a few dresses and ordered them made to our sizes and in our respective colours. Once again the driver was waiting for us and he took us to another shop where Mistress Joanna selected some lingerie and nighties. We left with several bags and some more orders placed.

Finally we got back into the car and were driven home. We sat close together on the back seat of the car, my head resting on Joanna's shoulder, kissing her neck gently and stroking her breast through her soft satin blouse as Julie stroked me through the front of my skirt and my panties.

The driver carried our bags into the house then Mistress Joanna dismissed him and led the two of us to the bedroom where we continued kissing in various combinations as we collapsed together on the huge bed. Mistress Joanna leant back against me, rucking her skirt up and opening her legs so Julie could crawl across the bed to begin licking her through her satin panties. I kissed her neck and shoulders, caressing her breasts from behind as I unbuttoned her blouse and slid my hand inside her bra to gently squeeze her rock hard nipple.

Joanna's hand reached back to where I was kneeling on the bed behind her and she began to caress me through my skirt and panties, making me moan softly as I nibbled on her ear. I could hear her breath coming in gasps as Julie used her tongue on her and her arousal just turned me on all the more. I cried out as Joanna's hand made me come in my panties at the same time as Julie brought her to orgasm between her legs.

Julie rolled onto her back and Mistress Joanna guided me to kneel and begin to lick her in the same way she had just been licking Mistress Joanna. Julie tugged her panties down and off so that I could get my tongue inside her, making her buck and moan on the bed. I began moaning between her legs as I felt Mistress Joanna unfasten the back of my skirt and tug it down to caress my smooth bottom through my panties as I licked Julie.

I felt Mistress Joanna climb off the bed and a few moments later she climbed back on, now completely naked. She straddled Julie, lowering herself onto her face and Julie began to lick Mistress Joanna while I licked her. I heard Mistress Joanna gasp as another orgasm shot through her, followed moments later by the start of Julie's orgasm under my tongue.

The three of us collapsed on the bed in our various states of undress, gasping for breath and sharing tender kisses and caresses as we recovered.

"You were perfect today, Jenny," gasped Mistress Joanna between gulps of air. "My two beautiful girls. You turn me on so much!"

"Thank you Mistress Joanna," we both breathed in unison.

After a few minutes, when we had our strength back, we clambered off the bed and helped each other into the new silk nighties we had bought today. I loved how mine emphasised my small breasts and the way my nipples – still hard from our activity in bed – poked through the front of it. Mine didn't look as wonderful as Joanna or Julie's though and, as I tucked my willy and that strange, confusing flap of skin beneath it into my new panties, I was struck by a similar feeling regarding my breasts. They weren't as large as the other two women's and there was something about them that felt like something was missing because they were to small but at the same time feeling that they shouldn't be there at all. That made no sense though, so I tried to ignore the odd feelings about my body as Julie and I prepared a light salad for us to eat, chatting and giggling together at the kitchen table as the three of us ate in our nighties with a glass of wine.

Things carried on like that for a few more weeks. I started wearing heels sometimes with my maid uniforms. Nothing too high and nothing that would damage the flooring but I soon forgot how strange that first time going out in heels had felt. I forgot all about any worries regarding the odd flap of skin beneath my willy. Joanna and Julie never remarked on it and I couldn't remember it being any different so I forgot about it, especially as it seemed to shrink a little as the weeks went by – or at least I thought it did, I could never be sure I was remembering things correctly and relied on Mistress Joanna and Miss Julie to help me whenever I was confused.

The confusion wasn't just about that though. I suppose it must have been because I was taking fewer of the pink pills. They had a sort of numbing effect on my thoughts as well as the effect of heightening my senses when being touched by Joanna or Julie. Without them, being touched by the two women or being allowed to touch them still felt amazing but I found myself crying more. I blubbed whenever

Mistress Joanna or Miss Julie were unhappy with me, I sobbed when they complimented me. I literally lay in bed crying thinking about how much I loved them as we snuggled in our beautiful satin nighties.

We went out more frequently and soon I forgot my nerves. There still seemed something not quite right about putting on my makeup and a beautiful skirt or dress to go out but I could hardly tell myself that it wasn't normal, could I? Every time the driver was waiting with the car to take us somewhere though, seeing him gave me an odd little shock, as if each time it reminded me that it was possible to be something other than a girl. I wondered what it must be like, to not be a girl; to wear those strange things round his legs that weren't a skirt. But my thoughts went fuzzy every time I pondered it and tried to work out why seeing him made me feel so strange – something halfway between a forgotten memory and a deeply hidden yearning to be more like him somehow. It felt oddly like there had been some sort of missed opportunity; that I had once had a chance to be something different, more like him but I'd missed that chance or had it taken away from me somehow. Seeing him made always made me think of that shrivelling flap of skin between my legs as if something had been there and wasn't any longer but I still couldn't work out what or why the driver made me think of such things.

Those thoughts never lasted long though. Either Julie took my hand and talked to me hypnotically as we drove somewhere or I forgot the driver as soon as we were back in the house where I had no cares or worries except to be a good girl and obey Mistress Joanna and make her and Miss Julie as happy as I could.

Dr Carol and Susan continued to visit. Susan was doing something to me that meant I gradually had to shave my legs and body less and less. It itched when she treated me but it was nice not having to shave so much, especially not having to shave my face. I'd never seen Joanna or Julie shaving their face so that was another thing t be glad of as I became more like them.

Dr Carol took a sample of my blood each time she visited and usually had me up in the stirrups to examine between my legs. One time I tried to ask her what she had done to me down there but she just smiled and said, "I just got rid of something you don't need any more."

"What was it? Was it something that was supposed to be there?"

She smiled again, her eyes twinkling with apparent arousal, "Not if Joanna didn't want them there, no."

"Is that flap of skin supposed to be there?" I asked. "It doesn't feel right."

"Don't worry your pretty little head about it, Jenny. If Joanna lets you keep this," I felt her touch my willy, "then the flap of skin will continue to shrink and you'll forget it was ever there."

I couldn't tell if that made me happy or sad.

Eight

Mistress Joanna had other visitors occasionally. Sometimes Julie and I served them in our maid uniforms and sometimes we socialised with them, dressed in our identical dresses but, as ever, mine pink and Julie's green in contrast to Mistress Joanna's habitual black clothing.

Some of her guests accepted me as her sister just as easily as they accepted Julie as her sister. I found it thrilling when people thought we were triplets – largely because I knew it made Mistress Joanna happy that she had so successfully made Julie and me into her doubles – but also because Mistress Joanna and Miss Julie were the most beautiful women in the world and they loved me so much that they had made me as beautiful as them. I couldn't imagine anything better than being a good girl for Mistress Joanna and pleasing her.

My confusions gradually diminished. The three of us getting dressed to go out together felt like the most natural thing in the world – three beautiful sisters helping each other into our lingerie and dresses, brushing each other's hair and handing items of makeup to each other as we sat together at the huge dresser getting ready in the mirror, our three almost identical faces beaming happily at each other.

Even seeing the driver and other men while we were out slowly stopped making me feel confused. If anything, I started to feel sorry for the poor driver in his uncomfortable-looking work clothes when I got to wear soft, comfortable satin maid dresses for my chores. What actually took longer to get used to was calling the women Joanna and Julie instead of Mistress Joanna and Miss Julie while we were out of the house. I felt a little guilty at not curtseying when Joanna gave me an instruction in public but it was what she wanted and I wanted to make her happy. It felt amazing being treated as almost her equal when we were out of the house but it felt right to obey her and be a good girl for her when we were at home.

There was one time that was an exception to the rule of appearing to be her equal outside our home. I was serving Mistress Joanna a cup of tea and Julie had gone to fetch the post. She came back looking very excited indeed and handed an ornate envelope to

Mistress Joanna. Joanna opened it with a grin and read it while Julie bounced on her toes in excitement.

"What is it?" I asked.

"An invitation to Mistress Delilah's party!" exclaimed Julie. "It is, isn't it Joanna?"

"Yes girls, it's an invitation."

Julie squealed and hugged me. "We get to show Jenny off!" she cried, hugging Mistress Joanna as well.

"Who is Mistress Delilah?"

"One of my old school friends," replied Joanna. "And one of the select few people who knows about Julie and you. She holds a party every year for people with…unusual…tastes."

Julie was still bouncing with excitement, "People are going to be SO surprised to see Jenny. Especially when they find out she used to be a b…" she glanced at me, "…when they find out what she used to be."

I looked at her in confusion, "When they find out I used to be a what?" For the life of me I couldn't work out what she could be alluding to. She grabbed me and kissed me roughly, forcing her tongue into my mouth and making me forget what I had been asking. I melted into her arms, sliding my arms round her neck and surrendering to her kiss and getting hard in my panties.

She broke the kiss, leaving me gasping and hanging weakly from her shoulders as she grinned at Joanna, "Sorry, I'm just so excited."

Mistress Joanna lifted her leg up on the sofa and started to hike her short black silk skirt up, "Oh no, you two girls carry on. I love watching you kiss. I can't wait to show Jenny off to people."

Julie started kissing me again, one arm gripping firmly about the waist as her other hand caressed my sensitive breast through my satin dress, making me moan against her lips and get even harder in my panties. Her arm round my waist pulled me tight to her as she rubbed her groin against my erection through our petticoats and satin skirts.

Julie's hand moved down from my breast to the front of my skirt, lifting it up and making me moan as her hand found the front of my panties under my dress.

"I'm going to make absolutely everyone touch this otherwise they'll never believe it's real!" she moaned as she rubbed me through my panties.

Mistress Joanna was touching herself through her own panties as she watched us. "And I can't wait until next year to show everyone how different she looks without it," she gasped as her fingers moved inside her lingerie to touch herself.

"What do you mean?" I asked in confusion but she just smiled as Julie pushed down on my shoulders. I got to my knees, kissing her beautiful thighs below the hem of her dress. She also knelt and pushed me further, making me lie down on my back.

I heard Mistress Joanna moan as she watched Julie push the hem of my dress up and begin kissing and licking me through the front of my panties, running her tongue the full length of my erection. My knees were up and Julie's long fingernails were caressing the backs of my thighs, pushing my legs wide to lick me through my soft satin panties. I lay there, gasping and moaning, helpless as I dug my hands into the thick carpet beneath me while Julie licked me.

I couldn't move, lying there in ecstasy as Julie licked me. I could barely concentrate enough to look down at her between glances at Mistress Joanna touching herself and writhing on the sofa. The sound of Mistress Joanna's orgasm made me come in my panties and I lay there gasping, knees still up in the air as my orgasm ran through me.

Julie got back up to her knees, one hand gently stroking me through my panties, making me gasp and shudder at her touch as her other hand went between her own legs and she began to touch herself just as Mistress Joanna had been. Julie was babbling and gasping as she touched herself, "I'm going to show your willy off to everyone. I'm going to show them how much of a girl we've made you and tell everyone what Dr Carol did to you. I'm going to show everyone how easily I can make you hard in your panties and…" she babbled on and on as she touched herself, her hand making me jump and shudder as she touched my erection, still very sensitive from the orgasm.

I heard Mistress Joanna have another orgasm, followed almost immediately by Julie's, with her still babbling about showing me off to her friends and how girly I was and how amazed everyone would be by what they had done to me.

It was a couple of weeks until the party and Julie seemed to be getting more and more excited about it. It felt like she was constantly putting her hand under the front of my dress to caress me through my panties, telling me how much she was looking forward to showing me off to everyone. I began to get a little nervous, unsure if she was serious about letting people I didn't know see or even touch my willy. I was still a bit confused by it, wondering if it was really supposed to be there; Miss Julie seemed certain that it should be and she loved it but Mistress Joanna seemed equally certain that it shouldn't be and that conflict just added to my confusion. I felt self-conscious about the odd flap of skin beneath it too – convinced that it at least was wrong, without being sure whether it was wrong in that it should be different or that it didn't belong. At least, as Dr Carol had promised, it seemed to be getting a little tighter and smaller so I hoped that it would sort itself out one way or the other.

On the morning of the party we awoke in our sexy little satin nighties and slowly made love to each other. As usual, I was only able to have one orgasm while the other two women had at least two as we kissed and licked and rubbed and caressed each other on the huge bed. With shaky legs and giggling like schoolgirls the three of us discarded our nighties and showered together in the wet room, still kissing and caressing each other as we washed one another and shampooed our hair.

We breakfasted together wearing just short satin robes and matching panties. Julie and I had chores to do but instead of changing into our maid dresses, Mistress Joanna made us remove our robes and put on a frilly satin half apron and a pair of heels so she could watch us work, both topless. I wasn't so keen on being topless as my breasts weren't as large or as pretty as the other two women's and gave me the same odd confusing feelings of them being either too big or too small without being able to work out which, just as the flap of skin between my legs did. Mistress Joanna loved seeing me like that though and the look of lust on her face and her touches on my breasts when I came near soon quashed any confusing thoughts with the intensity of the feeling her fingers on my soft flesh gave me. Seeing Julie topless and beautiful, also moaning in pleasure at Mistress Joanna's touches made it all the harder to worry about my breasts.

Julie and I spent a large part of the day like that – in just our tiny satin panties, aprons and heels, working to please Mistress Joanna as she sat watching us in her short black satin robe that gave tantalising glimpses of her own breasts and between her legs.

It was late afternoon when we started getting ready for the party. We went to our bedroom and sat at the dresser to do our makeup. Instead of all doing the same makeup, for once we did very similar makeup but in our colours – so I had pink eyeshadow and lipstick where Julie put on green and Mistress Joanna did hers in black. Next we painted our finger and toe nails in our colours and sat chatting as the polish dried.

Then it was time for underwear – matching of course – in our respective colours. Julie helped me into a beautiful pink satin corset. The weeks of massage and wearing one meant it fit perfectly without being uncomfortable. Quite the opposite – it made me feel secure and snug. It was padded and pushed my smaller breasts up so that when I had helped Julie into her dark green corset, our breasts looked almost identical. Then the pair of us helped Mistress Joanna into her black satin corset and we each put on matching satin panties. With our arms round each other's waists we checked our appearance in the full length mirror. Apart from the slight bulge in my panties we looked identical just in three different colours and I felt close to the two women, surprised how different I felt with breasts apparently the same size as theirs and not feeling out of place because of them being smaller. The effect was ruined slightly by the bulge in my panties growing as I looked at the three beautiful identical triplets in the mirror.

Up to that point I hadn't really given any thought to what I would be wearing to the party, assuming that it would just be a pink version of whatever Mistress Joanna chose to wear that night. So I was surprised when Mistress Joanna pulled two maid dresses I hadn't seen before from the wardrobe. Surely she wasn't going to dress as a maid as well?

"Are we wearing our maid dresses to the party?" I asked.

"Of course, silly," giggled Julie. "Mistress Joanna wants to show us off and let everyone see how submissive we are. You have to be on your best behaviour and make sure you don't do anything to embarrass her."

I frowned at the thought that I would misbehave in front of Mistress Joanna's friends. "Of course I'll behave! I'll be a good girl for you Mistress Joanna."

She gently stroked my cheek, "I know you will Jenny. I wouldn't be taking you out to show you off to everyone if I didn't know you would be a good girl."

I smiled, happy at her confidence in me.

Julie helped me into my dress. It was hot pink satin with white lace frills. It was a lot shorter than the maid dresses I usually wore as well as being lower cut. It felt like my knickers were barely covered and I was mesmerised by the site of my padded, lifted breasts being so visible at the front of the dress, unused to having cleavage. The sleeves of the dress were very short and puffed with a frill round them. The skirt was even more full than my usual dresses and the petticoats were so soft and flouncy against my thighs that they made the dress feel even shorter, though they also made the skirt flare out a lot more and feel a lot more swishy than I was used to. Overall the dress was sexier and a lot prettier than my usual maid dresses and it made me feel prettier too. The ones Julie and I wore most days were short and sexy but this felt a lot more like dressing up for something special. The apron was white satin with a pink satin frill and Julie tied it round my waist. The ribbons were a lot wider than my usual aprons and a lot longer and I could see in the mirror that she had tied it in a huge pretty bow and the ends of the ribbons hung down way past the hem of my dress, most of the way to the backs of my knees.

I helped Julie into her identical dress in dark green satin then we put our shoes on – patent leather with about a three inch heel in colours that matched our dresses. The heels were a little higher than I was used to but I had been wearing heels around the house occasionally and when we went out so they didn't give me any problems as I stood and looked at myself in the mirror, absent-mindedly swishing the full skirts of the dress around my thighs as I studied myself, amazed at how beautiful and sexy I looked and how different the low cut dress and the visible cleavage made me look and feel.

"Stop admiring yourself, girly," laughed Julie, elbowing me in the side. A little flustered, I apologised and turned away from the mirror, finding the sight of my identical twin just as alluring in her dark green satin dress, her bosom rising and falling as she breathed. Julie clipped a pink satin headpiece to my curly red hair and fastened a matching green satin one in her own hair.

We both turned to Mistress Joanna and curtseyed. She smiled, "Stunning. My beautiful girls!" We both blushed and curtseyed again, thanking her then helped her to get dressed.

Mistress Joanna was definitely not wearing a maid dress and I felt a slight pang of disappointment that I wouldn't get to see her in a sexy black satin maid dress that matched ours, even though it would have felt a little wrong to see her wearing such a thing as if she were a servant like Julie or me.

The dress she had chosen was black of course, in a shiny satin that was a lot heavier than the light flouncy dresses Julie and I were wearing. She stepped into it and we pulled it up for her to slip her arms into the sleeves. There were tiny satin-covered buttons all the way up the back of the dress which Julie and I fastened. The dress itself was ankle length with a full skirt but no petticoats. It had a tight bodice and a high neck with a black lace frill round it. The sleeves were puffed but full length, ending in a cuff with several more small satin-covered buttons.

Joanna sat and lifted her skirt up so we could place the knee length boots on her feet and fasten the buttons on them. They had a spike heel, about three inches the same as ours. When we finished and stepped back, she stood and smoothed the dress down. My jaw dropped – she looked amazing. There was something very Victorian about the way she looked and the black of her dress, makeup and nail polish just made her curly red hair and blue eyes all the more striking in contrast. With the ankle length dress, full length sleeves and high collar, Mistress Joanna was probably the most covered up I had ever seen her but also possibly the sexiest and most powerful-looking I had ever seen her. She quite literally took my breath away and I felt like dropping to my knees and worshipping her.

Julie gripped my hand and I could feel her trembling as we looked at Mistress Joanna, feeling small and helpless under her imperious gaze.

"How do I look, girls?"

Julie let go of my hand so we could both grab the hems of our short dresses and curtsey.

"Beautiful!" I gasped.

"Breath-taking!" I heard Julie gasp at the same time.

Joanna smiled, accepting the compliments as her right. "You both look beautiful too. I'm going to be proud to have everyone see how you've both turned out. I know you'll please me and be on your best behaviour in front of my friends."

"Of course, Mistress Joanna," I curtseyed.

"Maybe..." I heard Julie begin hesitantly next to me. "Maybe you should give me a spanking just in case, to make sure I behave..."

Joanna smiled indulgently and sat on the stool at the dresser. She patted her knee, "Of course, my darling."

Julie, looking like she was having trouble standing, blushingly approached Mistress Joanna and draped herself across her lap, her dress short enough to expose her panties slightly as she did so. I stood there watching, hands clasped in front of me as Joanna lifted the short skirt of Julie's dress and gently pulled down the back of her panties. Julie was breathing heavily as Joanna raised her hand, paused then brought it down hard on Julie's bottom with an audible slap. Julie gasped, half in pain and half in pleasure and I gasped in unison, feeling myself hardening in my panties.

As Joanna delivered several more hard spanks to Julie's rapidly reddening bottom my erection continued to grow and I gasped at the same time as Julie did with each spank. The sheer power radiating from Mistress Joanna was exhilarating and I had butterflies in my stomach. For the first time ever I wanted to be the one being spanked, wanting nothing more than to feel the helplessness of being over Mistress Joanna's lap, feeling her hand on my bottom.

My knees were weak and my erection was throbbing as Joanna gently caressed Julie's bottom before pulling her panties back up and smoothed the back of her dress down. Julie carefully climbed to her feet, dropping a curtsey, her voice trembling as she said, "Thank you Mistress."

"You're welcome, my love." Her gaze turned to me and I felt my knees nearly give way as my erection twitched. "Do you think you need a spanking too, Jenny?"

I bobbed a nervous curtsey, and whispered a barely audible, "Yes Mistress."

My nipples were hard in the cups of my corset and my legs had trouble obeying me as Joanna smiled and patted her knee. I managed a clumsy curtsey as I approached, gulped and lay myself across her lap, my erection pressing hard against her thighs as I felt the back of my dress sliding up. I gasped as I felt Joanna's hand lifting the hem of my skirt, certain that I was about to orgasm right then at the touch of her fingertips on my satin-clad bottom.

She tugged at the back of my panties but the erection at the front was stopping them from sliding down. I heard Mistress Joanna laugh, "They appear to be caught on something. Not to worry, that won't stop me spanking you. But we will have to get rid of that troublesome little thing sooner or later, won't we, Jenny?"

"Yes Mistress," I whispered, too turned on and feeling too submissive and helpless and desperate for her spanks to say anything to disagree with her. I lay across her lap and the mixed anticipation, longing and fear of her hand made the half second pause stretch out unbearably. Her hand came down and I gasped and shuddered on her lap, the sudden stinging pain taking my breath away. Several more spanks landed on my bottom, each just as hard as if she had been punishing me for something. The feelings it gave me were different though – instead of shame and tearfulness at being naughty and making her punish me I felt owned and submissive, utterly helpless at the power of this amazing woman.

I jumped at the gentle touch of her hand on my bottom as she caressed it and smoothed the back of my dress down. I only just managed to climb off her lap and stand on my trembling legs, my bottom still tingling and hot as I attempted a shaky curtsey and thanked her.

Julie was holding my hand again as Mistress Joanna stood and smoothed her dress down. She studied us and all we could do was gaze back in adoration, still holding each other's hand and trying not to collapse.

Joanna smiled, "I've got something else for you both to wear tonight." She opened a drawer and pulled two satin and lace items from it; one pink and the other green, matching the fabric of our dresses. She walked round behind me and I felt her reach round me. I realised that she was fastening a collar round my neck, or a satin and lace choker. I watched as she did the same to Julie, wondering why there was a small metal ring at the front of the collar. That quickly became clear when Mistress Joanna attached a long green satin leash to the front of Julie's collar then attached a matching pink one to mine.

She stood in front of us, holding the ends of our leashes and smiling at us. "Perfect. I think we've got time for a quick drink before we leave. Come along, girls."

She turned and Julie and I followed her submissively, on the end of our leashes as she led us downstairs. I was still hard in my panties with my bottom still tingling from the spanking, feeling shaky and overwhelmed by Joanna but desperate to please her and secure in feeling owned by her. Despite the confusing things about my body and the vulnerability the short, low-cut dress made me feel and the nervousness about Julie's insistence that she would be letting people see or touch my willy, I felt safe belonging to Mistress Joanna and was grateful to her for looking after me and caring for me.

As we made drinks for ourselves, Joanna popped a little pink pill into my mouth. I wondered why, as this was the first time she had given me one for days, perhaps even for a couple of weeks.

Julie was seemingly getting excited about the party again. We sat on the huge leather sofa, Mistress Joanna still holding the ends of our leashes as Julie babbled on about showing me off to people and how amazed they were going to be when they realised what was in my panties.

Suddenly she gasped as an idea occurred to her. "Can we tie Jenny up?" she asked Mistress Joanna. "I want to tie her hands behind her back so she can't stop anyone who wants to lift her skirt and see what's in her panties!"

Mistress Joanna's eyes were twinkling as she considered the suggestion. I gaped at her, not sure I liked the idea, worried by the thought of complete strangers lifting the front of my short dress while I was helpless to resist.

Joanna pondered for a few seconds then a huge smile spread across her face, "That's a wonderful idea. You don't mind, do you Jenny?"

"I…" I couldn't bring myself to disobey her at all. I could feel the pink pill addling my thoughts a little but the warm tingling in my bottom and the vision of beauty that was Mistress Joanna were all I wanted to concentrate on anyway.

She smiled and looked back at Julie. "Go fetch a pink silk scarf from upstairs."

Jenny leapt to her feet with a huge grin as Mistress Joanna let go of her leash. "Yes Mistress!"

She turned to leave the room in excitement but Joanna added, "Bring a green one too."

Julie turned back to her, pouting slightly. "What for?"

"If Jenny is going to be tied up, it's only fair that I tie you up too."

"But I wanted to lift her skirt to show people! How can I do that with my hands tied behind my back?"

Joanna's smile got bigger. "Your hands will be tied in front of you. Jenny won't be able to stop anyone I allow lifting the front of her dress to see what's in her panties...and you won't be able to stop anyone lifting the back of your dress if they want to spank you."

Julie gasped, "Yes Mistress!" she curtseyed and hurried from the room.

Joanna looked at me as she swallowed the last of her drink, seeing how nervous I looked.

"Don't be scared, Jenny. You're mine. You don't have to worry about anything. There's nothing you can do about it so just relax and obey me and enjoy yourself. You won't be keeping it for much longer so don't worry about people seeing it tonight, they probably won't get another chance so there's no need to be embarrassed."

"I won't be keeping what?" I asked in confusion, trying to work out what she was talking about, the effects of the pill making it hard to concentrate on anything that wasn't Mistress Joanna. The panties I was wearing? This dress? I was a bit worried about people seeing my willy but mostly hoping they didn't laugh or think I was too weird for that odd flap of skin down there. Maybe that was what she meant – it was already shrinking so she was reassuring me that it was going to go away completely, perhaps.

Julie returned before I managed to work out what she was talking about or ask any further questions. Mistress Joanna allowed me to finish my drink then ordered me to stand and put my hands behind my back. She tied my wrists tightly together with the silk scarf Julie had brought down. She didn't tie them too tight – they weren't uncomfortable – but I could tell that it would be impossible for me to get my wrists free without help. I stood there as Joanna tied Julie's wrists in front of her then, with a mischievous grin flipped the back of Julie's dress up, making her squeal and wriggle. It was futile of course, with her hands tied in front of her like that, there was nothing she could do as Mistress Joanna lifted her dress and delivered a sharp spank to her bottom.

"What a wonderful idea, Julie," grinned Mistress Joanna.

"At least I can still use my hands for most things," said Julie with an equally mischievous grin as she reached out and lifted the front of my dress. It was my turn to squeal and wriggle helplessly with my hands securely tied behind my back and completely unable to stop her lifting my dress and touching me through my panties.

"This is going to be SO much fun!" giggled Julie.

Joanna glanced at the clock. "Time to go, girls. Come along." She took the ends of our leashes again and led us into the hallway where she put a dark fur stole round her neck and hung a small satin bag over the crook of her elbow. Leading us by our leashes she opened the door and led us outside where the driver was waiting by the car.

If he was surprised to see two sexily dressed maids with their hands tied being led on leashes, he didn't show it at all, just held the door for us as we climbed into the car, me struggling a little with my hands tied behind me. I sat and Mistress Joanna pulled the seatbelt across me and clipped it into place then did the same to Julie. I wasn't uncomfortable on the large padded seat but it felt a little strange and made me feel helpless and vulnerable, particularly with the way Julie was still just about able to reach her two tied hands into my lap and caress me through my panties as the driver climbed into the front seat and pulled away.

With the effects of the pink pill and the things Julie was saying – telling me what a pretty girl I was, how happy I was to obey Mistress Joanna, how lucky I was to be a girl like them – while she touched me through my panties, I paid no attention to where we were going or how long it took to get there. I just came mostly out of my daze as Joanna said, "We're here," and leaned forward to unclip our seatbelts.

It was a struggle getting out of the car and with my hands tied behind my back there was no way I could keep control of my skirts. As Julie and I stood there, Mistress Joanna smoothed down our dresses and gave us each a long kiss on the lips. "Come along, girls," she said as she took our leashes and led us towards the main door of a house which, if anything, was even bigger than our own from what I could see of it. The sounds of music and laughter could be heard coming from the house.

We entered the house and a smartly-dressed maid welcomed us and took Mistress Joanna's stole. Her uniform was a lot more utilitarian than mine and Julie's; it was black cotton with no frills, elbow length sleeves and came to her knees. It didn't even have any petticoats. I felt sorry for her having such a boring uniform and was glad that Mistress Joanna gave me such nice things to wear for her when I served her.

The maid showed us further into the house and as Mistress Joanna led us through a large doorway my jaw dropped. I would have just stood and gaped if a tug on my leash from Mistress Joanna hadn't made me stumble after her as I looked around. There were maybe fifty people there already, in such an array of clothing that I couldn't at first make any sense of what I was seeing, my eyes leaping from one incomprehensible sight to the next. People were dressed in all sorts of things. I saw someone dressed head to toe in leather and zips, someone else dressed as a pink bunny rabbit complete with sexy lingerie, women and men in corsets and stockings and panties and high heels, several people entirely naked, one of them with a tail like a horse. Julie and I weren't the only maids, neither were we the only people on leashes. There were people with ball gags and handcuffs and I saw two women hogtied on the floor with bright scarlet ribbons, both blindfolded and licking the feet of a woman standing over them wielding a whip. My brain couldn't take it all in.

Moving through the room were several more of the smartly-uniformed maids, their no-nonsense outfits almost making them stand out in this amazing crowd and making it obvious that they were staff, not guests.

"Lady Joanna!" I heard someone exclaim and I tore my eyes away from the sights around me to see who had spoken. Joanna was smiling at a tall middle-aged man wearing a Zorro-type eyemask, what looked like a gladiator kilt and very little else.

"Hello, your honour," she replied. He glanced at Julie and me, raising an eyebrow as he said, "And hello Julie," to neither one of us in particular, obviously unsure which of us was Julie. Julie giggled and bobbed a curtsey, "Hello Sir."

The man looked intently at me while talking to Joanna, "You seem to have...ah...acquired another double, Lady Joanna."

Feeling very nervous under his stare but not wanting to embarrass Mistress Joanna in front of her friends, I also bobbed a curtsey.

"This is Jenny," smiled Joanna.

"You'll never believe what she looked like when we met her!" enthused Julie. Before I could protest she grabbed the front of my dress and lifted it as high as she could. With my hands tied behind my back there was nothing I could do to push it back down and I didn't dare pull away from her. All I could do was stand there blushing furiously as the man looked at my panties then did a double take and looked more closely.

"I say! Is that real?"

"Of course," replied Julie. "You can touch it if you don't believe me."

I gulped as the man leered at me, "Perhaps later." He looked back at Joanna, "What on earth made you decide to turn a boy into your double?"

"It was Julie's idea. I wasn't convinced but Jenny has turned out far better than I hoped."

Julie dropped my skirt and I breathed a sigh of relief, too glad that the man hadn't taken Julie's offer to touch my willy to be paying much attention to what they were saying.

"I've promised to let Julie keep Jenny's little thing for now. I couldn't help myself though, I had to have something done down there."

"Dr Carol?" asked the man with a grin.

Joanna nodded.

"There's a woman who really enjoys her hobby," laughed the man. "Did the poor boy mind?"

I looked up at the mention of Dr Carol. Were they talking about what she had done to me? Did this man know about it? What had they been saying? I hadn't been paying enough attention. I'd vaguely registered that they had been talking about Joanna doing something to a boy and now this man was talking about Dr Carol doing something to him but I had completely missed which boy they were talking about.

"Oh no. I don't think she even fully realises what has happened to her. Not that she'd have been given a choice either way."

The man looked back at me, his grin growing even wider, "How delicious!"

I frowned, becoming more confused again. Now they were talking about a girl. I couldn't keep up.

"I am very impressed, Lady Joanna. You are an artist. Well, enjoy your evening," he looked pointedly at me, "*girls*. I need a drink. We'll chat some more later."

Joanna and the man air kissed and he strolled off, waving and hallooing someone else he knew.

With a tug on our leashes, Joanna led us across the room, greeting various people as she went. She led us towards a tall black-haired woman who was talking with a group of people. She turned as she saw Joanna approaching and her face lit up as she hurried over to us. Joanna and the woman embraced, sharing a long kiss. "So lovely to see you again, Jo," smiled the woman.

"You too, Dee." The woman glanced at Julie and me and smiled widely at Julie, "Hello, Julie my dear. You look stunning."

Julie curtseyed with a smile on her face, "Thank you Mistress Delilah, so do you."

Then the woman turned to me and smiled, "And you must be Jenny. Lovely to meet you, dear." Her face lit up as she smiled, her piercing green eyes twinkling with merriment as she studied me. She had long black hair, left loose and eye-catching red lipstick. She was wearing a fishnet body stocking, extremely high heels and a large strap-on dildo.

"I must say, Jo has done an amazing job on you. You look just like her."

I smiled and curtseyed, pleased at the compliment and how thrilled Mistress Joanna looked by it. "Thank you Mistress Delilah."

She studied me some more, walking slowly round me, "Simply amazing. I would never have believed it was possible." I stood there blushing as she inspected me, almost jumping when I felt her breath on the back of my neck, "Do you realise how privileged you are to belong to Joanna, my dear?"

I tried to curtsey, "Yes Mistress Delilah." I felt her hands on my hips, caressing me through the satin of my dress. Her hands moved up and started to move round to the front. As she got closer, I gasped as I felt her strap-on lift the hem of my skirt and press against my bottom as her hands found my breasts through the front of my dress.

"Are these real, Jenny?"

"Yes, Mistress," I whispered, confused as to what else they could be. "They're not as big as Mistress Joanna's though."

"Shame. I'm sure she'll do something about that. Are you glad the hormones are working?"

I wasn't sure what she meant. I remembered there had been some conversations at home about hormones, especially when Dr Carol was there but, as with so much else, I didn't really understand everything that had been said.

"I'm not sure. I think so. I don't really know what they are."

"Well," she breathed in my ear, still fondling my breasts and pressing her strap-on harder against me, "you don't need to worry about it. Dr Carol has made sure they'll work as well as they can."

I still didn't know what she meant but I nodded, "Yes Mistress Delilah, Dr Carol helped make me prettier for Mistress Joanna."

She removed her hands and stepped back round in front of me, looking at Joanna again. "I still can't quite believe that she used to be…I wouldn't believe it just looking at her."

"I can prove it!" giggled Julie. "And you can see what Dr Carol did if you want?"

"That sounds like a wonderful idea, Julie. Why don't we all have a seat and a chat a bit later and you can show Jenny off to me?"

"Of course!" grinned Julie.

"But for now you'll have to excuse me. There are more guests to greet. Go enjoy yourselves and we'll continue this a bit later." Joanna and Delilah kissed again and Delilah moved off.

With a tug on our leashes, Joanna led us to get drinks. She greeted more people, most of whom called her 'Lady Joanna'. Julie took every opportunity to lift my dress and show people what was in my panties, to either great surprise or impressed congratulations. Despite the intense embarrassment of people looking at or touching my willy in my satin panties, I couldn't help but get a little aroused at the look in Mistress Joanna's face as she talked to people about me and how happy Miss Julie looked. Both of them were clearly thoroughly turned on and knowing that I was making them happy was turning me on too. I kept getting hard in my panties when Julie reached under my dress to touch me and that only made the embarrassment worse when she lifted my dress to show someone. All I could do was try to avoid eye contact and look around me at the bizarre display of people at this party.

We stood for a while as Mistress Joanna chatted to an old friend, a man in his 30s wearing a mint green ballgown who had a younger man kneeling at his feet with a leather hood over his face, leather shorts that appeared to be padlocked to him and a studded dog collar and leash, also padlocked. Mistress Joanna was holding our leashes as she chatted to her friend.

Julie got drinks for us both. With her hands tied in front of her, she had no trouble drinking but with my hands tied behind me, I couldn't hold a glass so she put a straw in it and giggled as she watched me having to bend forward to drink from the glass on the table. I knew that every time I bent forward, my short dress lifted to expose my panties but there was nothing I could do about it and it felt so good when Julie fluffed the back of my dress and caressed my bottom through my satin panties that after the first few times I didn't care, just enjoyed her touches and her arousal at seeing me like that. She was showing my panties and what was in them off to everyone she wanted to anyway and I was not the most revealingly dressed person there by any means.

We mingled for a while longer and ended up kneeling obediently at Mistress Joanna's feet while she sat chatting to another friend for a while. This friend was a young-ish woman who was with a man of about the same age as her. He was dressed as a baby, in a very short frilly pink gingham cotton dress with a matching bonnet. He had cute little pink Mary-Jane shoes and pink frilled ankle socks. He also had a dummy in his mouth that was fastened round his head with a pink leather strap and what appeared to be padded mittens on his hands except they had no thumbs and it was clear that he was almost as helpless with his hands like that as I was with mine tied behind my back. As he sat on her lap, his girlish dress was short enough to see that he was wearing a nappy and he nuzzled the woman's neck as she chatted to Mistress Joanna.

Of course, Julie insisted on showing the woman what was in my panties, kneeling in front of me so she could reach with her tied hands to lift my skirt and pull the front of my panties down so that she could see properly. The woman smiled, "How pretty! So small and cute," as she reached out to stroke it, making me blush even harder. The man on her lap frowned as he watched her stroking me but with his gag and mittens he was just as helpless as I was. He was also just as vulnerable, as the woman proved when she tilted him backwards on her lap a little and he wriggled and protested feebly as she pushed up the hem of his dress and carefully unfastened his nappy. She pulled the front of it down and we could see that he also had a willy but his was locked inside some sort of clear plastic contraption. Whatever the thing was, it would obviously stop him getting an erection. "I love it!" enthused Mistress Joanna. "Perhaps we should get Jenny one of those."

Julie pouted and Joanna laughed.

"Does it stop him getting hard?" Joanna asked the woman.

"Of course. And he can't touch it properly. Not that he would be able to with his mittens on anyway but it just makes extra sure that my little girly behaves himself and doesn't try to play with it. It keeps him well behaved. A week or so in that as punishment and he would do anything to get me to take it off and touch him."

"I don't think I'd like that," said Julie, still holding up the front of my dress. "I like Jenny being able to get hard. We have a collar that we can make her wear if we don't want her touching herself down there."

"Does she still get hard?" asked the woman. "I can see you've had Dr Carol take care of her. I was thinking about letting her do her stuff to my little girly here." She looked down at the man on her lap, making cootchy-coo noises at him, "Would baby like that? Would baby like me to get Dr Carol to cut his little balls off?"

The man looked worried and shook his head, unable to say anything to protest through his gag, just looking at her pleadingly as she smiled and made baby noises at him.

I wasn't really paying attention. I just stared at the thing on the man's willy, thinking how uncomfortable it looked and surprised to see a boy with a willy dressed as a girl. I started thinking again about my own body. I had a willy too. So far it was only boys I had seen with a willy – this boy here and a few naked men at the party. So why did I have one? I was a girl, wasn't I? I frowned with the effort of thinking through the haze of the pink pill. I couldn't be a boy. I had breasts and the boy on the woman's lap had odd round lumps under his willy while I just had that strange flap of skin. Had Dr Carol done something to try to make me look more like a boy? Why would Joanna want that? So far I had been feeling embarrassed by my willy; every time Julie showed it to someone I got a faint twinge of regret that I had it and wasn't as perfect as Mistress Joanna. But now I was just confused about why it was there at all. People had been saying some odd things – did I used to be a boy? That didn't seem right but neither did having a willy and I was becoming more convinced that only boys had those. My head was starting to ache with the odd thoughts going round and round and I tried to push them away.

The woman looked back at Joanna, "I hadn't told him yet but I'm seriously considering having him done. Was it easy?"

"Oh yes," replied Mistress Joanna. "It only took her about half an hour. Then it was a few days of recovery. You won't regret it."

The woman smiled back down at the young man on her lap, "What do you think, girly? Snip-snip and get rid of them? Would baby like that? Would he?"

The man was shaking his head, eyes wide as he tried in vain to mumble through his gag.

"Aw, baby is scared. Never mind, you won't miss them, will you baby? Would baby like to stay in his ickle cage for another month until he begs me to let Dr Carol cut them off? Would he? Yes he would. He would let Dr Carol cut his little balls off if I promised to throw the cage away afterwards, wouldn't he? It won't stay on once your balls are gone anyway so you won't ever have to wear it again if you're a good little baby and beg nicely."

The man was still shaking his head but the woman smiled, "That's what we'll do. We won't take your little cage off tonight after all, we'll leave it on your ickle thing until my little girly begs me to see Dr Carol, won't we? Yes we will."

The man was mumbling into his gag ineffectively as the woman gently refastened his nappy, still cooing about keeping his cage on until he was a good little girly and begged her to see Dr Carol.

"You'll have to let me know how it goes," grinned Mistress Joanna as the woman cuddled the feebly protesting man against her again, straightening the front of his dress and rocking him on her lap.

"I might even invite a few friends round to watch it being done. It's so much fun how much he cries and begs to be let out of his cage after just two or three days. it. When he was very naughty once I kept him in it for nearly two weeks and he was absolutely frantic by that time. He's been in it for just over a week to get ready for this party and I did promise him that I'd take it off tonight." She grinned down at him, "I promised to take your little cage off tonight if you were a good little girly, didn't I. But we're not going to do that now, are we? Baby is going to stay in his ickle cage until he begs to be snipped by Dr Carol, isn't he?"

She looked back at Joanna, ignoring the man struggling on her lap, "I reckon a month more in it and he'll be begging me to have his balls cut off." She glanced back down at the man in the baby dress, talking to him as well as Joanna, "And if he takes too long to be a good baby and beg, then I might make him keep his little cage on for a few extra months before he sees Dr Carol."

We mingled some more and I forgot my confusion about my willy, wondering why the woman's baby man was so scared of Dr Carol. Whatever she had done hadn't harmed me and it made Joanna and Julie very happy indeed so I couldn't guess what he seemed so scared about. Probably the thought of being in that cage for a long time, not about Dr Carol. I shuddered at the thought of being locked up like that without being able to get hard or feel Joanna or Julie touching me.

The party had been in full swing for a couple of hours now. It was obvious that people were moving off into other rooms to have sex. Some were staying in this main room and doing so, although normal sex didn't really seem to be happening. The two women I'd seen hog-tied earlier now seemed to be tied to each other, licking each other between the legs as people watched and touched themselves.

A while later we bumped into Mistress Delilah again. "There you are, Jo. Having fun?"

"Definitely!"

"Let's sit somewhere quieter and chat and you can tell me more about Jenny. I can see that Julie has been showing her off to everyone she can all evening."

She summoned one of the staff maids and ordered drinks and we followed her to a quieter alcove where there was a large sofa. Delilah and Joanna sat down with Joanna still holding mine and Julie's leashes. Delilah crooked a finger and Joanna tugged my leash. I curtseyed and stood in front of Delilah. She sat forward and gently pushed up the hem of my skirt, looking at me through my panties for a long moment. "Unbelievable," she muttered, shaking her head while Joanna grinned, looking very pleased with herself.

Delilah stroked me through the front of my panties and I blushed, feeling utterly helpless and vulnerable and mortified that I could detect the stirrings of an erection due to the touch of her hand on my willy through my satin panties. With one hand holding up the front of my dress, she used the other to ease the front of my panties down. She let the dress drop as she put her other hand under it and hooked her thumbs through the waistband of my panties, tugging them down almost to my knees. She pushed the front of my dress up again and her hand caressed my naked willy for a moment before moving it out of the way to look underneath it.

My face was burning and I couldn't look at Delilah. Julie was grinning like a lunatic watching what Delilah was doing to me and Mistress Joanna was leaning close to Delilah, also looking between my legs and obviously proud. I glanced around, feeling like my blush got even worse as I noticed several of the other partygoers looking over at what Delilah was doing.

Her fingers slipped between my legs, caressing the odd flap of skin. I could feel my willy stiffening slightly despite the embarrassment.

"Wow, they feel so different when they're empty!" she said as she caressed the flap of skin between my legs. "This seems tighter than I was expecting. Did Dr Carol take some of the skin away?"

"No," replied Joanna, "It's just shrivelling a little now there's no use for them."

"Wonderful." She was still caressing me between my legs and I could feel myself getting hard.

"I see it doesn't stop her getting an erection?"

"It was a small risk but worth it. And Julie's happy about it."

"Definitely!" beamed Julie. "And it was such a turn-on watching it happen. Seeing Dr Carol at the end of it with them in her hand, knowing that it was so final and permanent as she made the last cut. I nearly came right then."

"Does she still get hard just as easily as she used to before it?"

"Yes!" Julie knelt in front of me and her hands reached under my dress, making me gasp and moan as she stroked my willy, making it even harder. I blushed at the stares of others nearby, watching me as I stood in my little maid dress with my panties round my knees and Julie's hand under my petticoats. Mistress Joanna and Mistress Delilah relaxed back in the sofa, watching as Julie caressed me. I wriggled but my hands were still firmly tied. I was completely hard now, the growing erection brushing against the soft petticoats of my dress only helping speed the process that Julie's hands had begun. I moaned softly as she continued to stroke me, using both hands as they were still tied together in front of her.

"I can make her hard any time I want and there's nothing she can do to stop me," said Julie as she continued to rub my erection with her hands. "This little thing belongs to me now. It's not hers any longer."

I saw Mistress Delilah's hand creep into Joanna's lap and start to tug at the front of her skirt, pulling it up. Joanna's hand went round Delilah's shoulder, draping across her and touching the top of her breast through her body stocking.

Julie pushed the front of my dress up further now and my knees went weak as her head went under my dress and her lips touched my erection. Delilah had pulled the front of Joanna's dress right up now and it was bunched on her lap with Delilah's hand slipping under it and between Joanna's legs, Delilah's other hand absently stroking the strap-on in her lap as they watched what Julie was doing to me.

It was as much as I could do to concentrate on not falling over as Julie kissed and licked my erection, the front of my dress pushed right up round my waist now and what she was doing to me clearly visible to anyone who happened to glance over.

Julie's lips were around my erection now, her tongue running along the underside of it. Joanna had her head thrown back on the sofa, her eyes closed and making sexy noises at Delilah's touch between her legs. Delilah's hand on the strap-on was rubbing it up and down now, pressing it against herself in time with Julie's head moving on my erection. I heard Joanna let out a long moan as she bucked on the sofa, pressing her thighs tight around Delilah's hand as she came. The sight of the woman I worshiped in the throes of ecstasy like that brought on my own orgasm and I came in Julie's mouth, her tongue still caressing me as I gasped and spurted.

Julie sat back on her heels as my orgasm finished and I fell to my knees, too weak to stand any longer, still gasping and shuddering in the afterglow of my orgasm. I leaned forward, lying against the sofa next to Delilah so that I didn't fall over any further, oblivious to the fact that my bare bottom was now sticking up in the air, my panties still round my knees. Joanna was smiling happily, caressing the hand between her legs as Julie shuffled forward and gripped Delilah's strap-on, rubbing it with both hands. Delilah let go of it and leaned back, watching Julie. I lay there against the sofa, still gasping and breathless, shivering as Delilah's free hand caressed me through the back of my soft satin dress while Julie pressed the strap-on against her until she too let out a moan and started writhing on the sofa in orgasm.

When she got her breath back a little, Delilah reached forward and caressed my bare bottom, making me gasp again. "Would you like to borrow the strap-on, Julie? Jenny looks so pretty and tempting like that."

Julie grinned, "No thank you."

I was still on my knees, lying forward across the sofa with my hands behind me as Julie straddled me. I gasped again as my fingers touched her between her legs, caressing her through her panties. She wriggled on me, making me press into her. I tried to push the edge of her panties out of the way so I could get my fingers inside her and I knelt there, bare bottom exposed to everyone, pinned face down on the sofa as I brought Julie to her own orgasm, straddling me with my fingers inside her.

When she finished using me, she climbed off me and tugged the back of my panties up, helping me back to my knees as she tugged them all the way back into place then helped me onto the sofa and the four of us sat there panting and getting our breath back. Joanna and Delilah shared a long kiss while Julie and I did the same then the two of us collapsed back on the sofa, leaning against each other as Joanna and Delilah kissed and chatted. I nearly fell asleep, snuggled against Julie in our maid dresses.

I was awoken by Julie kissing me again and saying, "Wake up, sleepy head."

I blinked and smiled at her, struggling into a more upright position and wriggling my arms as much as I could with them tied. I had fallen asleep for a while and was starting to get pins and needles in my arm. The party seemed to be winding down a little. Apparently quite a few people had made their way to bedrooms to carry on their activities. I yawned and looked around. The lights had been dimmed and I could see shapes moving together as more people had sex. Joanna and Delilah were standing and kissing as they embraced, apparently saying goodnight to each other. Delilah thanked us for coming and said, "It was a delight to meet you, Jenny. I still can't quite believe what an amazing job Jo has done. You're a lucky girl."

"Thank you Mistress Delilah. I *am* a lucky girl. And thank you for inviting us tonight."

She gave Joanna another kiss and wandered off to talk to someone else. Joanna also yawned and smiled at Julie and me. "I think we'll call it a night, girls. Poor Jenny looks exhausted. Let's go home and get into our nighties."

I struggled off the sofa, Julie helping me, and Joanna took our leashes to lead us from the room, saying goodnight to various people as we left and stepping over several combinations of people enjoying themselves on the floor.

A maid returned Joanna's stole and the driver was waiting for us outside. I was almost asleep again by the time we arrived home and had to be helped out of the car by Julie. Joanna led us by the leashes back into the house and up to our bedroom, where she unfastened our collars then untied our hands. I rubbed my wrists, glad to be free again but feeling a little odd about it, like something wasn't right, not being tied up and helpless and vulnerable for Mistress Joanna.

Julie and I helped Joanna into a long black satin nightie then helped each other undress and into our green and pink matching nighties. We snuggled together in huge bed, the feeling of the two beautiful women's bodies against me in our gorgeous satin nighties making me feel safe and secure. I was fast asleep within moments.

Nine

More time passed in our huge beautiful house. It was large enough that there were always plenty of chores for Mistress Joanna's adoring maid doubles and I loved how happy she was whenever we pampered her and how pleased she was by how tidy we kept the house for her. We even got to wear the maid dresses she had bought for Delilah's party at home sometimes and it always fascinated me seeing my own cleavage, as well as arousing me seeing Julie's as we worked. Mistress Joanna also often chose tops or dresses for us to wear that showed off our cleavage and I noticed that I sometimes seemed to have cleavage even without a bra, just in one of my tiny satin nighties. I wondered why I had never noticed that before. I supposed that I must have always had that and laughed at how silly I had been before when I worried about not being the same size as Mistress Joanna or Miss Julie. True – mine weren't as big but they still looked pretty in my nightie or in a tight pink satin blouse.

We went to other parties occasionally but nothing like Mistress Delilah's. I was presented as Joanna's sister and felt a little thrill whenever people accepted that we were identical triplets as there could be no greater compliment than people thinking I was as pretty as Joanna or Julie. I was in heaven whenever the three of us stood with our arms round each other's waists, admiring our triple reflection in the mirror, wearing our identically-styled but differently coloured outfits as we got ready to go out somewhere.

I lost all track of how long I had been with them. I suppose it must have been a while because summer turned into autumn and winter. I remember how pretty it made me feel when Mistress Joanna bought us matching padded jackets to wear. I felt a little guilty thinking it but I thought that mine, in bright pink, was far prettier than Julie's green one or even Mistress Joanna's black jacket. With its figure hugging shape that emphasised my curves and the luxurious fur-edged, satin-lined hood, I felt so girly when I wore it fastened tightly with the hood up, my beautiful red curls spilling out of it.

I saw men while we were out of the house, of course, but gradually they stopped making me feel so nervous and confused. I spent most of my time in satin and frills with two amazingly beautiful feminine women, and men just seemed so…sort of rough and uncouth compared to us girls. I didn't like the attention we got from them whenever we were out somewhere but Mistress Joanna and Miss Julie were very good at deflecting them and protecting me. I couldn't even really remember what had been so confusing about men a while ago. Something about not being able to remember if men had willies or just women. Some women anyway. But I didn't dwell on it.

To be honest, half the time I forgot that I even had one, except when something happened to remind me, like seeing it in the shower or Joanna or Julie doing something that made it get hard. It was most noticeable when the three of us were in short satin nighties with no panties but usually we were doing things to each other that swiftly took any confusion or concerns about it away. The odd flap of skin between my legs continued to tighten and shrink until it almost vanished. I couldn't quite recall how big it had been before but I was pretty sure that it had worried me. Now I hardly ever thought about it. It did seem to me that my panties felt a little more comfortable but I wasn't certain. Julie seemed pretty sure that I looked a lot prettier in my panties now, so I took her word for it and stopped worrying or trying to work it all out.

I was never quite sure if Mistress Joanna had a job but she occasionally spent the day away from the house, leaving Julie and I to our chores. Less frequently, she stayed away for a day or two. I missed her terribly at those times but Julie seemed to enjoy being in charge and was far more likely to find an excuse to spank me for something when Mistress Joanna was out. On the other hand she was also far more likely to find an excuse to kiss me and put her hands up my dress and we often abandoned our chores for a while as we kissed and fondled each other to orgasm in our maid dresses. And even when she did spank me, it usually led to the fondling and kissing afterwards anyway.

We always made sure we hurried to complete out chores afterwards though, not wanting to disappoint Mistress Joanna or give her a real excuse to spank one or both of us. Not that she needed an excuse. If she felt like spanking one of us, then she did so. Sometimes she liked to watch Julie spanking me. I barely even noticed that I never got to spank Julie. Of course – neither of us ever spanked Mistress Joanna.

We had a wonderful Christmas. Julie and I had a chance to go out shopping together one day while Mistress Joanna was away. We chose some lovely presents for Mistress Joanna and chose things for each other, careful not to look at each other's purchases and spoil the surprise.

We spent an entire day putting up Christmas decorations, under Mistress Joanna's supervision. A lot of the time was spent giggling and kissing and touching each other as Julie or I climbed the stepladder to put up a decoration, knowing that the other two could easily see her panties under her short satin dress and petticoats. Julie loved making me squeal when she touched my bottom through my panties as I climbed the ladder or reached to place a decoration. No matter how many times she did it, it made me squeal girlishly and blush.

On Christmas Day, Julie and I were given satin outfits to wear that were a cross between a sexy Miss Santa costume and a maid dress, in red satin with white fur trim and a very short skirt, lots of petticoats and low-cut to show off our cleavage. This was the first time I recalled wearing red – I sometimes wore a black skirt or a white blouse or something similar with my pink clothes but no other colours. I had my pink satin underwear underneath it but even so it felt a little strange. It was nice being dressed exactly the same as Julie, except when I got glimpses of her green silk panties.

It was a lovely day, chatting and kissing as we prepared the huge dinner, giving each other presents, Mistress Joanna sitting in her large chair in front of the fire as Julie and I handed them out. Unwrapping our gifts and thanking each other, enthusing about the things we had been given. Finally falling into bed in our nighties, exhausted and happy and eager to cuddle and touch each other.

Winter turned back into spring and my entire life consisted of Joanna and Julie. I could neither remember nor imagine anything different.

One day, when Joanna was away again, I was tidying a guest bedroom as a few of Mistress Joanna's friends were going to be staying over in a few days' time. Julie was somewhere else, tidying a different room. I hadn't really been in this room much before – there were so many in the house and there were quite a few that we never actually used. I had been in here a few times with Julie, just dusting and vacuuming, keeping it tidy. This time I was getting it ready for guests so I made the bed and did an extra thorough job of dusting and cleaning, opening the windows to make sure it was properly aired and checking drawers and the built-in wardrobe, making sure clean towels and a bath robe and a new toothbrush and toiletries and so on were on hand to make sure everything was tidy and ready for Mistress Joanna's guests to use if they wanted to.

The chest of drawers was empty so I put scented pouches in them and turned to the wardrobe. There were a few things in there – mostly older winter clothes which I moved towards the back to leave space at the front in case the guest in this room wanted to hang any clothes.

There was a box on the floor at the front and I pulled it out and put it on the bed to see what was in it so I could decide what to do with it. When I opened it I was surprised to see a set of men's clothes. They were a little scruffy and much cheaper than anything we wore. Maybe they'd been left behind by a past guest who had stayed here. I folded them carefully in case he ever came back for them and as I did so I noticed a few other things in the box. There was a watch and a pair of shoes and a wallet. It didn't feel quite right poking through someone else's things but I thought I should probably have a quick look to see who these things belonged to so we could return them if he didn't know they were here.

I opened the wallet and pulled out the driving licence. The name seemed really familiar for some reason and I struggled to recall where I knew it from. It was a fairly common sort of name but the surname had a slightly unusual spelling and I had a vague thought, about how annoying it was to have someone spelling it incorrectly even though they had seen it written down. Why would I think that? And why did the name seem so familiar but so unfamiliar at the same time?

I looked at the photo on the licence. The man looked familiar too. I couldn't quite put my finger on why. Had I met him before? The name felt familiar but not like I knew him as a friend or something more like…more like I had only told his name to other people for some reason or heard other people saying his name but not calling him by it myself. And the picture – I could almost remember seeing his face but again it didn't feel like I had talked to him or known him as an acquaintance. I had the strangest feeling that I had mostly seen his face while he had been shaving or brushing his teeth but that didn't make any sense. Perhaps he was an actor or something and I had seen him in an advert. Looking at the licence and the paltry pile of clothes was making me feel very odd indeed.

I didn't like how it was making me feel. It was almost like looking at the belongings of a dead man or knowing that something terrible had happened to the person who owned these things but not knowing what that was. A shiver ran down my spine and I began putting the things back in the box, wanting only to hide it in the wardrobe and forget about it.

"What are you looking at, Jenny?"

I jumped and turned at the voice behind me. "Mistress Joanna! I thought you were going to be out all day." She looked stunning, wearing her hair held back with a black silk Alice band and wearing a long black satin robe that was loosely tied. It looked like she only had lingerie on underneath it.

I curtseyed, "I was just getting the room ready for your guests and I found this box. Who is this?" I showed her the driving licence and she smiled.

"Nobody important. I forgot those were there. I meant to get rid of them."

"Won't he want his things back?"

She shook her beautiful head, "No. He doesn't need them any more."

"He…he's not dead, is he?"

She laughed, "No. He's very happy. He just doesn't need those things from his old life any more." She put the things back in the box and closed it, setting it on the chest of drawers. "I see you've been a good girl, doing your chores."

"Yes Mistress Joanna," I curtseyed.

She smiled and held up a pink pill. She pressed it to my lips and I obediently swallowed it.

"Do I look beautiful, Jenny?" she asked.

I curtseyed again, "Of course Mistress Joanna. You always look beautiful." I could feel myself starting to get hard in my panties as I drank in the sight of her, her intense gaze making my knees go weak. There was a strange look on her face, or perhaps she had done her makeup slightly differently from usual.

"My beautiful, submissive girl. My sexy little maid. You look so beautiful in your pretty pink satin."

"Thank you Mistress Joanna," I was definitely getting harder now, pleased at her compliments and once again becoming aroused by knowing that she had made me as pretty as she was.

She stepped closer to me and I was trembling as her hand caressed my cheek. "Do you love me, darling Jenny?"

"Yes Mistress Joanna, more than anything!"

She moved closer and planted a gentle kiss on my lips. "And do you worship me?"

"Yes!" I breathed, unable to tear my eyes from her perfect face as her other hand moved to the front of my dress, gently stroking my breast through the satin. Her hand on my cheek moved to the back of my neck and she pulled me in for a longer kiss, her tongue sliding into my mouth as my lips parted and I moaned softly. My nipple under her thumb was as stiff as my erection in my panties and an electric thrill ran through me as she flicked her thumbnail against it.

Her hand move down from my breast to my waist, pulling me closer against her, my erection pressing against her through the flimsy black satin she was wearing. Involuntarily, my arms slipped round her neck and I melted into her embrace as she kissed me deeply.

We kissed some more and she tipped her head to the side so I could kiss her perfect neck, carried away by the feeling of my breasts pressing against hers and her hand on my waist making me feel small and owned. I mumbled random nothings about how beautiful she was as I kissed her neck and felt her groin pressing hard against my erection.

Gradually she moved me back towards the bed as we kissed. I could feel the effects of the pink pill starting, making her every touch feel like electricity and all coherent thought dissolving in a cloud of love and adoration for her.

I gasped as she moved me further back and the edge of the bed against the back of my legs made me sit down suddenly. "Mmmm," she moaned as she bent forward and pushed the hem of my dress and petticoats up my thighs. She reached down to touch me through my panties as I caressed her through the thin satin robe, able to feel that she did indeed only have lingerie on beneath it. I lifted my bottom off the bed as she pulled my panties down and off. She fluffed my dress and petticoats over my erection, making me moan and shudder at the feeling.

She straightened up and slowly untied the sash of her robe, pushing it open so I could see that beneath it was a black silk and lace teddy. Her knee pushed mine apart so she could step closer again, her thighs tantalisingly close to my erection. She sighed and pushed her chest out as my hands reached up to caress her breasts through the soft black silk. We were both breathing heavily, lost in each other as she tugged the sash from her robe and dropped it on the bed, then let the robe slip down off her shoulders and fall to the floor so that she was standing between my legs in only the black silk teddy.

"Worship me with your mouth, my darling girl," she whispered as she pulled my head forward between her legs. I willingly obliged, kissing and licking her through the silk as my hands caressed the backs of her smooth, firm thighs and her silk-clad bottom. I reached to unfasten the bottom of the teddy but she pushed my hands away.

She held my head tight against her as licked and kissed her and soon I could hear her gasping as her orgasm approached. "Not yet, Jenny," she gasped, pulling back from me. "Lie on the bed."

I did as she ordered, moving back on the bed and smoothing my dress and petticoats down over my thighs. Joanna climbed on the bed and straddled me, leaning forward to kiss me roughly, my head held in both hands and her groin so close to my erection that I wanted to scream and beg.

She took both my wrists and pushed them up over my head. Then she reached over to grab the sash from her robe and quickly tied my wrists to the bed. I let out a long moan as she wriggled down my body, only petticoats and skirt separating my erection from entering her. I wriggled but I knew that Mistress Joanna never wanted to use my erection like Julie did and I groaned in frustration.

With a smile she reached between her legs and unfastened the bottom of her teddy. I stared in astonishment, hardly daring to hope that at last Mistress Joanna wanted me to enter her. She started pulling the hem of my dress up. I wanted to touch her but my hands were securely tied to the bed. I let out a cry of pleasure as my erection sprang free from under my dress and she pushed down, making me enter her.

I writhed on the bed beneath her, beyond ecstasy at the feelings of Mistress Joanna using me for her pleasure. As she thrust up and down on me, I gazed lovingly at her face, wishing that I could reach up and touch the perfect breasts I could see jiggling beneath the black satin. With a shout, Joanna came, pressing down hard against me and moaning. The spasms of her muscles around my erection bringing me close to my own orgasm.

"WHAT THE HELL IS GOING ON HERE?"

I cried out in frustration as Joanna scrambled off me before I could come. I turned to see who had shouted and was stunned to see Mistress Joanna standing in the doorway. She was wearing a long black leather coat with a black silk blouse and black satin pencil skirt. She looked furious, with her hands on her hips staring at us. I turned my head in confusion to see Mistress Joanna next to me on the bed, looking scared and starting to apologise. I looked back to the doorway but Mistress Joanna was there too, still looking furious and stepping towards the bed.

The Mistress Joanna who had just entered was staring angrily the Mistress Joanna on the bed next to me. I looked back and forth between the two of them, gradually realising through the haze of the pink pill's effects that the woman on the bed with me was Miss Julie.

"What are you doing?" Demanded Mistress Joanna. I struggled with my tied wrists but it was no use. Fortunately she wasn't looking at me. I opened my mouth but nothing came out, completely speechless and unable to think of anything to say to apologise to Mistress Joanna. I felt sick at the thought that this might be my fault, that I might have done something to make her this angry or get Julie into trouble.

"I'm sorry, Mistress Joanna," Julie was pleading. "I just wanted to feel more like you. I wanted Jenny to worship my like she worships you." She was cowering on the bed looking close to tears.

"She already does worship you, you stupid girl. You can have sex with her whenever you want. But how dare you pretend to be me? How dare you wear my things?"

"I just wanted her to think I was you, to feel like you. Please forgive me Mistress, I didn't mean to make you angry," Julie was sobbing now, tears running down her face as she begged forgiveness.

"Get that off right now. You wear green. I wear black, not you."

"Yes Mistress," cried Julie, scrambling quickly off the bed and taking off the black silk teddy.

"I'm so sorry Mistress. I'll never do it again. I just wanted to feel what it was like to be you. Just once. I'm sorry."

Joanna still looked furious as she watched Julie remove the teddy and kneel before her, naked and begging in tears. I lay there, forgotten, feeling very vulnerable and helpless with my hands tied and my dress rucked up round my waist with no panties on. Mistress Joanna didn't seem angry at me though and the two women paid me no attention whatsoever.

"This is unacceptable Julie."

"I know. I don't know what I was thinking. I knew it was wrong, I just wanted to feel like you so desperately."

Joanna sighed and sat down in the armchair in the corner of the room. "Maybe I'm partly to blame. Turning you into my double and making you want to be like me."

Julie sniffed back her tears, "I'm sorry Mistress. This was all my idea and my fault."

"Look at me."

Julie looked up at Mistress Joanna and wiped a tear away. She was still sobbing and more ran down her cheeks.

"You will be punished for this."

"Yes Mistress. I know. I deserve to be punished."

"You really do." Joanna patted her knee and Julie clambered to her feet, obeying Mistress Joanna and draping herself across her lap. "We'll start with a spanking."

Julie screwed her eyes shut as Mistress Joanna raised her arm, "but don't expect this to be your entire punishment, my girl."

Julie's 'Yes Mistress' was cut off by a sudden squeal as Joanna's hand landed hard on her naked bottom. I winced – I could tell that she'd hit her really hard. Much harder than usual. She raised her hand again and spanked Julie several more times, each smack sounding loud in the room, even louder than Julie's cries of pain or the sobs in between the spanks. Her bottom was bright red after only a few spanks but Mistress Joanna kept going, the blows too hard for her to sob or cry out even, she just lay there gasping and gulping for breath as the spanks rained down on her, turning her bottom and upper thighs bright red.

After what seemed an eternity, Mistress Joanna finished spanking Julie, who lay limply on her lap, shuddering and still gulping for breath, her tears starting again and a drained moan escaping from her lips. I was crying too, partly at the sight of Julie being so severely spanked and partly in distress that Mistress Joanna was so upset.

"Th…thank you Mistress," gasped Julie, weakly.

Joanna's frown relaxed a little and she caressed Julie's sore bottom, making her wince. "Don't think that thanking me gets you out of any further punishment. That was just to make the point while I thought about how else to punish you."

Joanna looked thoughtful then looked up at me. "Look, you've upset poor Jenny too."

"I'm sorry Jenny," whispered Julie. "I shouldn't have tricked you like that."

I wanted to tell her it was okay but it wasn't. She had seriously angered Mistress Joanna and I couldn't tell her it didn't matter when doing so would mean me disagreeing with Joanna. There was no way I wanted a spanking like that. Despite my sympathy for Julie, I felt a relieved that Joanna wasn't also angry at me. This was probably still my fault somehow but Joanna was blaming Julie and I couldn't work out what I had done to cause this so I kept my mouth shut in case I made things worse. Maybe if Joanna…I mean Julie…hadn't given me the pink pill I could have worked out what to say but the only thought I could cling onto was that Mistress Joanna needed to be pleased and obeyed so that neither of us got punished even more.

"How do you think I should punish Julie for being so naughty, Jenny?"

I just stared at her, frozen between wanting Julie's punishment to end and wanting to obey Mistress Joanna. "I…she…" I burst into tears again. "I don't know."

Mistress Joanna looked thoughtful then smiled widely at me. "I know. I think I should take away Julie's favourite toy. Don't you think that would be a suitable punishment, Jenny?"

I blinked away a tear and looked at her in confusion. I couldn't think what Julie's favourite toy could be. "I…suppose…"

"Jenny, no!" cried out Julie. She cried out in pain as Mistress Joanna gave her another hard spank.

"That's quite enough from you, Julie."

"Well Jenny? Should I take away Julie's plaything or think up another punishment? Maybe I should spank her some more while you think about it?"

I looked at Julie who was staring desperately at me and shaking her head, pleading with her eyes. I didn't know what she was trying to communicate to me. Did she want me to disagree with Mistress Joanna or was she begging me not to make Joanna think up a worse punishment? All I was certain of was that I couldn't bear to see her spanked any more.

"Please don't spank her any more! Take her plaything away!"

Joanna beamed at me and I breathed a sigh of relief that she didn't raise her hand again. "I've wanted to do that for ages and I think now is the time to finish what Dr Carol started. I'm glad you agree, Jenny."

"Please don't!" begged Julie. "Jenny…She means she wants to cut off your…"" she clamped her mouth tight shut as Joanna raised her hand again.

"Please don't spank her any more, Mistress Joanna! She's sorry she tricked me and sorry she pretended to be you. I know she is."

"So we've decided, have we Jenny? We're going to get rid of her plaything?"

I still didn't know what she was talking about but this seemed like a way to end Julie's punishment. I couldn't stand to see her spanked any more and I hated the thought that Joanna would come up with something even more unpleasant for her. I didn't know what this 'plaything' she was talking about was but having a possession taken away couldn't be any worse than the spanking and surely Mistress Joanna would relent and let her have it back once she'd calmed down.

Julie was still frantically shaking her head at me. I tried to smile to reassure her but she was whispering, "No, no, no, no, no!" The silly woman was too distraught to realise that I was trying to help her.

"Yes Mistress Joanna," I said. "You should take her plaything away. Don't punish her any more than that, please?"

Joanna beamed at me but Julie was wriggling on her lap, crying again and begging, "Please don't do this Joanna. She doesn't understand. Please!"

"Shhh," Joanna hushed her. "It's decided now. No more arguing or I will think of something else as well."

Joanna helped Julie off her lap and made her kneel by the chair. She came to sit on the bed next to me. "Don't cry, Jenny dear. This is for the best. You'll see." Her hand began to caress my thigh. Julie just stared, looking distraught but obedient.

"Thank you for helping me to decide on her punishment, Jenny. It's not so much of a punishment really. I'll be happier. I think you'll be happier too. And Julie will be when she gets used to the idea, once it's done and there's no going back." Joanna's hand moved further up my leg, touching me gently. Her fingers found the strange ridged patch of skin beneath my willy that I vaguely remembered being a flap of skin before it tightened. I gasped at her touch, desperate for some tenderness and affection after everything that had just happened and eager for Mistress Joanna to be less angry and forgive Julie.

I trembled as she touched me and despite the strong emotions of seeing Julie spanked and being so confused at everything else that was going on, I felt my erection stirring again.

"I think getting rid of it is the right thing to do. Girls shouldn't have such things anyway. Only boys have them so it's only right to get rid of it, isn't it?"

I still didn't know what she was talking about but it seemed to make sense so I nodded, "Yes Mistress Joanna. Girls shouldn't have things that are only for boys."

"Good girl. I'm glad you agree. If you had something that only boys were allowed to have, something that meant a girl couldn't really be a girl, you'd want me to get rid of it for you, wouldn't you?"

"Of course, Mistress Joanna. I want to be a good girl for you."

"You are, Jenny. And you're going to be an even more perfect girl for me and Julie will just have to learn to live without it, won't she?"

Her tenderness and her touches were definitely making me hard now and I moaned softly as she spoke to me, the haze of confusion and the heightened sensuousness caused by the pink pill making it hard to do anything but agree with her and writhe beneath her hand, tied to the bed and at her mercy as my erection grew and I couldn't concentrate on anything but her hand on it. The memory of thinking that Julie was her and about to let me enter her mixed with the wonderful feeling of her stroking my erection, which was also something she very rarely did, mostly letting Julie play with it as Julie was the one who liked it so much and Joanna didn't.

"Do you think I should forgive Julie once I've got rid of it?"

"Yes Mistress!" I gasped, struggling against the satin sash securing me to the bed and wriggling under her hand.

"Yes, I think I will but she's been so naughty that I don't think I'll even let her have one last chance to play with it. Part of her punishment can be watching me play with it for the last time it ever gets used. Does that sound fair, Jenny?"

"Yes!" I gasped, not really listening as my orgasm approached. Julie was still kneeling, staring at Joanna's hand on my willy with tears running down her cheeks and I smiled at her again, happy that her punishment was nearly over. I moaned again as I felt myself passing the point of no return, Mistress Joanna's hand on my erection the most amazing thing I had ever felt. "Don't be sad Julie," I whispered to her. "Girls shouldn't be allowed to have boy things. You'll be happier when it's gone."

Julie looked upset but I forgot her as Joanna's hand finally made me come. I cried out as she continued rubbing me, making it last a little longer and caressing me gently as it finished. I lay there gasping for breath, still feeling Joanna's hand on my willy, amazed and pleased that she was happy to touch it so much more than usual and hoping that she would want to touch it lots more in future.

Ten

As I lay there gasping in the aftermath of my orgasm, Joanna stood and ordered Julie to her feet. Julie obeyed, still sobbing and glancing at my willy. Julie started to beg again but Joanna hushed her. "No more from you Julie. It's decided. I've still got a choice between a penectomy and vaginoplasty so don't make me any angrier than I already am. Another word out of you and I'll leave her with nothing there to play with at all."

Julie apologised profusely and followed her from the room. I lay there trying not to cry, all the stress of what had happened and the amazing sensations of Joanna touching my erection and relief at the ending of Julie's punishment leaving me overwhelmed and emotional. Joanna hadn't untied me so all I could do was lay there and wait for her return.

She came back a while later and untied my hands. As I climbed from the bed she said, "Julie has been sent to bed early in another bedroom. Clean yourself up, find some panties and come down to make my dinner. I need to make some arrangements."

I curtseyed and hurried to the bathroom to wipe myself. I found some clean panties and hurried downstairs to start preparing Mistress Joanna's meal. This was the first time I had done so by myself and I was too busy trying to make sure I got everything right to worry any more about Julie just then. I knew she'd miss whatever it was Joanna was going to take away from her but at least she wouldn't be spanked any more, or worse.

I took Mistress Joanna a cup of tea and she was on the phone, arguing with someone. "…sure you wouldn't want your wife seeing those photos and I *know* you don't want the police seeing the contents of my other file." She paused, listening and smiling as I placed her tea in front of her with a curtsey. "Yes I understand, but you don't really have a choice do you?" She listened again and I stood politely with my hands clasped in front of me, waiting to be dismissed, in case she wanted anything else.

"No…no…well of course this means I will have even more against you. That's how this works…No…" she glance up and saw me, waving me away with a smile. I left her to it and went back to the kitchen to continue cooking.

She came into the kitchen a while later. "Well, that's all arranged Jenny," she smiled. I smiled back, happy for her without really knowing what she was talking about. I was sure she'd let me know if she wanted me to.

We ate our meal then she made me put together a tray for Julie. I offered to take it up to her but Joanna insisted on doing it while I tidied. She sent me to get changed into a nightie then we snuggled on the sofa watching a film before bed.

It was strange to go to bed just the two of us. A couple of times while Joanna was away it had been just Julie and me in bed and that had been strange too but it was even more strange just me and Joanna. I must have pouted a little when Mistress Joanna got out my collar and began tying my wrists with the ribbons but she laughed, saying, "I've had my fill of naughty girls today. I just want to make sure you don't get up to any trouble tonight. I meant it when I said that *I* would be the one using her...plaything...for the last time ever."

I frowned, still not having any clue what plaything she was talking about and having no intention of touching it myself even if I knew where it was. Before I could worry about it too much, Joanna was kissing me, caressing me through my pink satin nightie. My hands were on her breasts, caressing them through her blouse and starting to unfasten the buttons so I could touch her through her black satin bra.

She shrugged the blouse off then turned so I could unfasten her bra for her. We kissed some more and I unfastened her skirt, having to crouch a little due to the ribbons holding my wrists. Joanna removed her panties and ordered me to kneel.

I obeyed and she stood in front of me, naked. I stared up at her perfect beauty, hard under my nightie as I looked at her.

"Do you like being pretty for me, Jenny?" she breathed.

"Oh yes, Mistress Joanna!" I replied, amazed that she even needed to ask.

"If you could be even more perfect for me, you'd want to, wouldn't you? If you could be even more like me?"

"Yes! Anybody would want to be more like you if they could! You're perfect!"

She took half a step forward, the curly red hair between her legs just millimetres from my face. I trembled, desperate to kiss her and lick her there. I almost swooned as her hand gently took the back of my head and pulled me forward. I buried my nose in the curls, my tongue eagerly darting out to touch her and feel its way inside her. Her gasps and moans were music to my ears as I licked, my hands stroking her soft thighs as I did so.

"I'm going to make you even more perfect Jenny. I'm going to make you even more like me. You'll be my beautiful girl forever," she carried on like that as I licked, her voice coming in stutters and gasps as I used my tongue. "You're going to be so beautiful when we do this, so perfect, so pretty and girly..." I pressed harder with my tongue, in time with her gasps then suddenly she was shouting out and gripping my head tightly so I didn't stop licking as she came.

Moments later she squeezed her thighs together and stepped back shakily.

She helped me to my feet and gave me a long kiss. "Thank you darling. You wouldn't believe how turned on I am at knowing what's going to happen."

She turned to fetch her own nightie and slip it on over her head. "What *is* going to happen?" I asked, confused.

She smoothed the satin down over her body and patted me on the cheek with a smile. "Let me worry about that," she said. "You just carry on being a good girl for me and I'll make you even more perfect."

"Thank you Mistress Joanna," I curtseyed, none the wiser but comforted that she had everything in hand, whatever it was.

We climbed into bed together and had another long kiss. I was still hard under my nightie and was hoping that she would want to touch my erection again but she made me turn away from her so we could spoon, her body pressed tightly against my back only making me remain hard. She was kissing and nuzzling the back of my neck and her hand draped over me held one of my breasts, a comfortable handful for her and she was gently caressing my nipple, keeping that as hard as my erection until I could hear her breathing slow as she dozed off behind me. With my wrists tied to the ribbons I couldn't reach to touch between my legs and my erection throbbed. The best I could do was raise my hands slightly, one hand on top of hers as it held my breast and the other gently touching my other breast through my satin nightie. It took me a lot longer to get to sleep than it did Joanna.

I awoke the next morning to a kiss from Joanna. I blinked and looked up at her standing over me, fully dressed. With a start I sat up, already apologising for oversleeping and not being in my maid uniform to make her breakfast. She put her finger on my lips. "I let you have a lie in Jenny. Julie has made your breakfast for you."

A moment later, Julie entered with a tray. I sat up properly in bed and thanked her.

"Go pack a bag, Julie. We'll need things for a couple of nights at least." Julie curtseyed and left the room and Joanna sat on the edge of the bed while I ate. I tried to ask her where we were going that we needed a bag packed but she waved my questions away. "It'll be a surprise. You just do everything you're told and you'll be even more beautiful for me, okay?"

"Yes Mistress Joanna," I smiled as I munched my toast.

I stayed in my nightie, collar and ribbons for most of the day. Julie prepared lunch for her and Mistress Joanna but I wasn't allowed any, just a small glass of water. I started to cry, wondering if I was being punished for something and distraught, not at being punished, but at the thought that I could have unwittingly angered Mistress Joanna. She cuddled me and reassured me. "I'm not angry at you Jenny but this is necessary. Nil by mouth for you today I'm afraid, Just treat it as if you're on a diet for the day. This is all to help you become even more perfect remember."

I wiped a small tear away. "Yes Mistress Joanna, thank you. You would tell me if I'd been a naughty girl, wouldn't you? I don't want to make you angry at me."

She gave me a tight hug. "I couldn't be happier actually." I smiled back and put my trust in her.

It was getting near evening when I was told to get dressed. "Are we going out somewhere?" We hadn't prepared an evening meal so presumably we were going to a restaurant. That was good – I hadn't eaten anything since the two slices of toast first thing this morning so I was famished.

For once we didn't dress in identical clothes. Joanna was wearing black leather trousers and a polo neck jumper, Julie wore a green shift dress and I put on a short pink suede A-line skirt and a white satin blouse. We were dressed far more causally than we normally would for the sort of restaurants we tended to frequent and I wondered where we were going. Julie gave me a pink pill and another small glass of water, which was a relief as my mouth was dry as well as me feeling hungry.

The pill was starting to take effect by the time we left the house and got into the car. As usual when the pill was doing its work, I wasn't really paying attention to where we were going and this time it was Mistress Joanna holding my hand and talking to me in her sing-song voice, telling me how pretty I was going to be, how happy I was going to be when I was perfect, how much I wanted to be more like her, on an on as we drove, putting me in a happy daze just listening to her voice.

We climbed out of the car in the grounds of a large building. It didn't look like a house. Neither did it look like a restaurant come to that. Perhaps a hotel. We went through to some sort of reception area where we were checked in by a woman in a smart uniform, white. I thought it was an odd choice as it made her look a little like a nurse, not a receptionist.

Someone led us to a room. There was a large bed with a strange frame. It clearly wasn't large enough for all three of us. I looked at Mistress Joanna questioningly as Julie laid out a pink nightie on the bed.

"We're not all going to fit in here are we?" I asked.

Joanna smiled. "Don't worry Jenny dear. This is your bed. Julie and I have the room next door so we can be close to you."

I felt tears spring to my eyes. "Did I do something wrong Mistress Joanna?" Why was I in a different room? Julie had been punished by being put in a different bedroom last night. Was I being punished now?

Joanna hugged me and kissed me. "Stop worrying. You haven't done anything wrong. Just relax and everything will be fine. I love you. This is all to help you be more beautiful."

"I love you too," I whispered, confused but comforted and willing to trust her. Julie helped me into my nightie and then a member of staff appeared to help me into bed. Joanna and Julie sat next to it and we chatted for a short while before a man wearing a white coat came in. I frowned – was he dressed as a doctor? I suppose that went with the women dressed as nurses. I didn't remember having to come to hospital for anything. Was this a weird theme hotel? I watched in growing confusion as Joanna stood and had a quick whispered conversation with him. The man didn't look happy about something but with a resigned sigh he approached the bed.

"Hello again Jenny."

"Hello?" I replied. I didn't remember meeting him before. Had I been here before? Perhaps he had been one of Joanna's guests at the house.

Joanna held my hand and smiled reassuringly as the man pulled the covers aside and began to push my nightie up. I wriggled and tried to push it back down but Joanna tutted and shook her head. "He just needs to examine you again Jenny. Don't worry about it."

I blushed and looked away as he pushed them hem of my nightie up round my waist and I had a sudden but very vague memory of being tied to the massage table at home with my legs up in the stirrups as this man examined me. It was just a quick flash and I wasn't sure I was really remembering it. I certainly couldn't remember when it was or why he had done so. Perhaps it was a follow up to what Dr Carol had done. I relaxed a little, trying not to jump each time I felt his hands between my legs. Dr Carol hadn't done anything to harm me and Mistress Joanna said she was going to make me even prettier so this must be linked.

After a while he pulled my nightie back down and placed the covers back over me. "We're set to start first thing in the morning. Everything you want done will take a couple of days. We'll keep her mostly out of it until we've finished. She hasn't had anything to eat today has she?"

"Two slices of toast at about 8am, a couple of glasses of water and one of her pills about two hours ago."

"That should be okay then. I'll go fetch the paperwork and I would appreciate it if you two stay out of sight in this suite. I'll have a meal sent up for you but Jenny mustn't eat anything and we need to be as discreet as possible. If anybody gets wind of what we're up to here…"

"Don't worry," said Joanna. "Just make sure you do a good job. There's a couple of your bosses who also know how to keep their mouths shut if I tell them to, so just concentrate on Jenny please."

The man frowned and left, shaking his head. He was definitely very unhappy about something but Joanna looked ecstatic. Julie however gave me pitying glances whenever Joanna wasn't looking.

Joanna sent Julie off on some errand and a short while later one of the staff who looked like a nurse came in with some equipment on a trolley. Joanna moved my bedcovers aside and the woman slid a mat under me. Joanna began touching me through the front of my nightie and I blushed wanting to push her hands away but not daring to as my erection stiffened while the other woman looked on.

When I was fully erect, moaning and gasping on the bed despite my humiliation at this happening in front of a complete stranger, Joanna pulled the hem of my nightie up then stepped back. I gasped and started to protest as the woman stepped forward and started smearing something from her trolley onto my erection.

"Shush Jenny," ordered Joanna. "Let her do her job."

"What's going on?"

Joanna giggled. "We're just going to make a copy."

"What do you mean?"

She giggled again at my confusion. "Never mind. Just a sort of consolation prize for Julie. For losing her favourite plaything."

I stared in bewilderment at her as the woman continued what she was doing. I couldn't make eye contact but her hands on it were keeping my erection stiff. She finished what she was doing and I was made to lie there with the white stuff on my erection as it gradually shrank, leaving the shape of the goo standing there. The woman carefully removed it and wiped me clean before pulling my nightie down. My erection had almost vanished by this time and Joanna was smirking as the woman left the room.

Julie returned a while later but Joanna didn't say anything to her about what had happened and I knew better than to mention it if Joanna didn't. Joanna and Julie sat on each side of the bed, holding my hands and we watched a film and chatted. I was allowed another sip of water but I must have drifted off to sleep because I don't remember seeing the end of the film.

I think I woke up a while later. It was light now, as if it were morning. There was one of the staff members who looked like a nurse and she gave me something to swallow from the tiny plastic cup. I was drowsy and still half asleep and it felt like my bed was moving but I either fell back asleep or it was just a dream.

There were other moments of near wakefulness but they were just a confusing jumble of impressions and sounds and I couldn't make any sense of them. They might also have just been dreams.

When I awoke properly it seemed like it must still be night. The lights in the room were dimmed. My mouth felt drier than ever and my throat was sore. I could see Julie sitting next to me and Joanna sitting across the room in a chair, reading a book.

I tried to say something to Julie but nothing came out. I gave her hand a weak squeeze. She looked round then smiled widely, "She's awake!"

They both jumped to their feet and Joanna came over to the bed, beaming her beautiful smile. "How do you feel Jenny?"

"Tired," I mumbled, my voice barely a croak. "And thirsty." Hardly any sound came out but Julie seemed to understand and she grabbed a glass of water from the table beside my bed. She helped me sit up a little so I could take a few sips. I realised that there was a drip attached to my arm and some of the lower part of my face was covered. When I touched it with my hand I felt bandages there and on my throat.

"What happened?" I croaked, my voice a little louder now that my mouth was wet but still barely more than a whisper.

"It was a complete success!" smiled Joanna. "You're going to be more beautiful than ever!"

I smiled back at her. Glad that she was so happy but too tired to ask what exactly she was happy about. I fidgeted to get a little more comfortable, wincing at an ache between my legs as I moved.

"Try to stay still Jenny dear," said Julie. You might be a little sore for a while but we'll do our best to keep you comfortable while you heal."

"Heal?" I whispered. Oh, that was right. Dr Carol was doing something to make me more pretty, wasn't she? Or was that someone else? I hoped she was getting rid of that strange flap of skin. I frowned. Hadn't that mostly gone already? Was it even really there to start with?

I must have looked troubled because Julie stroked my brow, smoothing my frown away. "Just get some rest Jenny. You've been unconscious for hours and now you need some proper sleep."

She helped me take another sip of water, for which I was very grateful. The man in the white coat came in and started to pull back my covers. I think I fell asleep again as he started to push my nightie up because I don't remember anything else until it was light again.

Nobody else was in the room when I awoke. I looked around and struggled into a sitting position. The odd ache between my legs made me wince again and it was matched by a similar but less painful ache in my chest. I reached over and grabbed the glass of water, draining it quickly. My throat felt like sandpaper and the water felt wonderful despite being room temperature.

"Hello?" I tried to call but my voice was hoarse and no louder than a whisper. It made my throat feel sore so I didn't try again. Someone would be in soon I assumed. I sat up a bit straighter, careful not to make the ache between my legs reappear. I looked down at my body. There were bandages round my chin and throat and chest beneath my pink satin nightie.

Carefully, I pushed the bedcovers aside and lifted the hem of my nightie. I was covered in bandages between my legs. There were thick elastic stockings on my legs and a tube coming from the bandages that ran off down towards the bottom of the bed. The drip was still in my arm.

I wondered what had happened. I wasn't in pain, just a few aches so I supposed I hadn't been injured. The pink pill had long since worn off so I didn't have so much trouble thinking. I still didn't know what had gone on but it was obvious enough that this was a hospital so whatever had been done to me was what Mistress Joanna had promised would make me prettier and more perfect. More like her. I smiled at the thought. There was a dull throb in my chin but no worse than you feel after going to the dentist for a filling.

I managed to pour myself another glass of water from the jug on the table and sipped it. If anything my throat hurt more than my chest or between my legs. I reached the remote and turned the television on. I could at least watch something while I waited for someone to come in. I didn't have to wait long. A few seconds after the sound began, the door opened and Julie bounded into the room. "Hello sleepy-head! How are you feeling?"

"Okay thanks," I whispered. "Little achy."

"I bet," she empathised.

Joanna followed her in and gave me a huge smile.

"Have you made me prettier for you, Mistress Joanna?" I asked.

Julie's face clouded but Joanna's lit up. "Yes my darling."

"What did they do?"

She grinned, "You'll have to wait and see when the bandages come off."

"Did they get rid of that flap of skin between my legs?" I asked, still half certain that it had vanished over time but unable to think what else they could have done down there. Just finished off getting rid of it I suppose.

Julie frowned heavily, turning away and folding her arms as if angry. Joanna put her hand to her mouth and giggled behind it, "Yes dear, that annoying little 'flap of skin' you had has completely gone. You'd never know it was there. In fact, a few pink pills and some suggestion while you heal and you might not even remember it being there at all."

"Oh. Good." My happiness at the obvious joy on Joanna's face mingled with a nagging notion that it shouldn't have been taken away, leaving me ambivalent. I didn't even know why I had that nagging feeling – all I could remember it causing me was confusion and uncertainty about my body. Should I be as happy as Joanna obviously was that it was gone now? And if so, why did Julie seem so unhappy about it?

Joanna and Julie refused to tell me what had been done to me. I was examined by the doctor a few times as the nurse changed my dressings. I wasn't allowed to look down there while they did so, Joanna ordering me to lie back and close my eyes while they did their jobs.

Later that day I was given another pink pill, so of course I stopped worrying about it at all, just happy to be with the two women and knowing that Joanna was so pleased with whatever she had arranged. Julie occasionally looked a little…not angry so much as wistful and resigned to something but she wouldn't say what was wrong and I assumed it was to do with her plaything being taken away by Mistress Joanna. I squeezed her hand comfortingly, glad that her punishment for masquerading as Joanna hadn't been worse. Joanna seemed to have forgiven her and didn't seem at all angry any more so I knew that Julie would be fine soon.

"Don't worry about losing your plaything," I tried to console her. "At least Mistress Joanna didn't punish you any worse than that. She might even let you have it back one day."

Julie shook her head, a mix of pity and amusement on her face. "Silly girl," she whispered, squeezing my hand and planting a tender kiss on my forehead.

Eleven

I stayed in the hospital for a few days before being given robe to put over my nightie, sitting in a wheelchair and being wheeled out to where the driver was waiting with our car. We drove home and I went straight to bed where I mostly stayed for a while longer. I suppose it was about a week although it might have been a bit longer. I was kept dosed up on the pink pills so I wasn't really keeping track of time.

Mistress Joanna had hired a nurse to come in and look after me and change my dressings. My voice came back after a day or so but it felt odd. Joanna gleefully told me that the doctor had done something to my throat to change my voice a little. It was strange hearing a different, slightly softer voice coming out of me and after a couple of days when my throat had healed properly I realised that my voice was a lot more like Joanna's now. It was bizarre at first but there was something nice about hearing her voice when I spoke.

The bandages came off my chin too. I couldn't tell what had been done but I was sure that my face looked a little more like Joanna's too. Whatever had been done was subtle and I couldn't feel any scar or see exactly what had changed no matter how hard I stared in the mirror. After a while I wasn't even certain that anything had changed even though it still felt nice to tell myself that I looked more like her now. I felt prettier because of it. Between the slight changes to my face and the change in my voice, it felt oddly like I was watching Mistress Joanna in the mirror whenever I was putting on my makeup and chatting with the other two, like I was inside her body controlling it or she was inside me looking out as I watched her move my hands and speak through me.

It wasn't long before the bandages on my chest also came off. Mistress Joanna had bought me a pile of new pink satin bras and of course she and Julie had bought themselves matching ones in black and green satin. We stood together, looking in the mirror, me still bandaged between my legs but Julie and Joanna in satin panties, admiring our new bras. Again I couldn't tell what had changed – my breasts looked exactly the same as theirs, so what had been done? I vaguely remembered that perhaps mine had been smaller but I wasn't certain; that could just as easily have been my own insecurity speaking.

I still wasn't allowed to see what was under the bandages when the dressings were changed. The tube had been taken out and I was allowed to use the toilet when the dressing was off – still without looking! The dressings looked a little odd under my nightie and I wished that I could be naked or wearing matching panties like the other two as we cuddled and kissed in bed, caressing, kissing and licking each other's beautiful breasts. It was frustrating sharing a bed and kisses and caresses with the two women. It was fun of course and there was nothing in the world better than seeing either of them in the throes of passion or feeling their perfect skin beneath my fingers or lips – but there was a tingly, aching longing between my legs. My nipples were hard and they paid them lots of attention but it was driving me wild that the dressings were in the way of them touching me between my legs in the same way I touched them or they touched each other. The fact that they were giving me several pink pills a day didn't help; every touch was driving me to distraction and I couldn't help but beg to have the dressings taken off so that I too could be touched. Julie spent hours caressing and licking my nipples until I couldn't take it any longer, what she was doing sending something very like an orgasm through me.

They also spent a lot of time talking to me in their hypnotic way. As always under the influence of the pills I hardly registered most of it – telling me how pretty I was how glad I was that Joanna had made me perfect, that I had always been a girl just like them, that I wouldn't even remember not being one of them, that when I saw what had been done to me I would be so grateful and happy, that I'd see that I had always been like one of them and had always been meant to be here as Joanna's girl, how much I was looking forward to having the bandages off so I could enjoy my body in the same way they enjoyed theirs. So much of it seemed to be too obvious to bother saying or seemed like a very strange way of putting things

Julie seemed to get over her unhappiness at her punishment. I was glad because I hated seeing her unhappy. Now she seemed to be getting excited at the prospect of my bandages being removed soon. If anything she was even more excited about it than I was. I was curious and I felt frustrated at being kept bandaged up like this but I didn't suppose that anything much had been done to me so I wasn't excited in the same way Julie was. She was acting as if there was something under them she had never seen before and was desperate to see what it was. Like a kid with a particularly intriguing

Christmas present under the tree that they weren't allowed to open yet. I tried to tell her that she was only going to be disappointed – Mistress Joanna had said that they just removed the annoying flap of skin. Obviously removing it took longer to heal than whatever Dr Carol had done to it. It's not like the loss if it was going to make much difference.

Finally the day came when my bandages were to come off at last! Mistress Joanna insisted on tying my wrists to the bed with pink silk scarves as the nurse lifted the hem of my nightie and removed the bandages. Joanna and Julie were watching closely. Joanna looked incredibly aroused and the sight of her was turning me on making my nipples hard and the area between my legs tingle. Julie was almost bouncing up and down in excitement.

She removed the bandages and examined me carefully. I had been given a pink pill so her hands between my legs was making me gasp and wriggle.

"She seems to have healed nicely. They did a great job." I could feel her prodding and poking me down there, stretching my skin.

"Is that…?" asked Julie, eyes wide as she stared between my legs, watching the nurse inspecting me.

"Yep!" grinned the nurse. "What's left of her…well you know. The surgical techniques have greatly improved in the last decade or so. It *should* be just as sensitive as it used to be. Almost as sensitive as your own clitoris."

A shock ran through me as she prodded me and Julie gasped almost as loudly as I did. I struggled to free my hands. Now the bandages were off, all I wanted was to feel Joanna and Julie's hands between my legs again. It seemed like it had been ages since I had felt them touching me down there. I moaned in frustration at the way my hands were tied. I strained to look down but as I was tied up, I couldn't move my head far enough to see past my breasts.

Julie just stood, staring between my legs in fascination as the nurse turned to speak to Mistress Joanna. I was too busy struggling with my tied wrists and begging Julie to untie me to pay much attention to what was being said. Something about being careful for a while, calling the doctor if there was any blood or pain, that I could use it but to be gentle for at least another few weeks.

Joanna thanked the nurse and ordered Julie to see her out. Julie took one last look between my legs with a huge grin and ushered the nurse from the room. Joanna sat on the bed next to, her beautiful smile washing over me. I struggled against the silk scarves again but she was making no move to free me. One of her hands moved between my legs and I tensed in anticipation, then gasped as I felt her fingers against me. I stopped struggling with the scarves binding my wrists and just lay there, moaning softly at her touch against me after so long without it.

"Does that feel good, Jenny?"

"Oh yes!" I breathed. She smiled and continued stroking me gently, her nipples hard beneath her blouse as she watched me writhe beneath her fingers. Her other hand started to unfasten her blouse and I moaned in frustration when she removed her hand from me to take the blouse off and remove her bra. I watched as she stood and went to her wardrobe, pulling out a small parcel and placing it on the end of the bed.

She unzipped her skirt, letting it fall to the ground. Julie came back in as Joanna removed her panties and he ordered Julie to strip too. Joanna sat back down on the bed, touching me again as Julie slowly removed her maid dress and underwear, placing them and Joanna's clothes carefully on the dresser without taking her eyes off what Joanna was doing to me. When Julie stood there naked, I could see that her nipples were just as hard as Joanna's or my own.

"I think we should untie Jenny now and let her see, don't you?"

"Yes Mistress!" exclaimed Julie, moving over to untie my hands and giggling prettily as I kissed the nipple that just about came within reach of my lips as she bent over me. I sat up as my wrists were freed and glanced down between my legs. There was nothing obviously strange there. The hair had been shaved and there was some light brown stubble. Joanna stood up and reached out her hand. I took it and got up from the bed. She removed my nightie and the three of us walked over to the mirror, standing arm-in-arm as we had so many times before, studying our reflections – this time in the nude instead of admiring our outfits.

I stared between the legs of my reflection, trying to work out what was different and comparing myself to Joanna and Julie. Apart from Joanna's curly red hair and Julie's blonde and my short light brown stubble, there was nothing obviously different about me between my legs. I reached down and felt further between my legs. The flap of skin had indeed gone and considering how small and pointless it had seemed, I was to be feeling that something a lot more important was missing. I stared at my reflection trying to work out what it was. My..w…no that didn't seem right. My thoughts got fuzzy as I tried to remember and I felt a little dizzy, clinging tighter to Joanna.

I looked back at Joanna and Julie. They didn't have anything I didn't so what could be missing? My…I realised I didn't really know what to call it, as if I'd never had to mention it to anyone before. That was odd. The word 'pussy' popped into my head but seemed a little vulgar for describing a part of my own body. I shook my head – it would come back to me, it was probably just the pink pill making me forgetful. Whatever I called it, it looked no different from Joanna's or Julie's. It must just be the lack of hair and the loss of that weird flap of skin making it look a little different from usual.

"Do you feel pretty Jenny?" asked Joanna.

I looked at my whole reflection, taking in all three of us. I looked almost identical to Joanna and Julie. Or more accurately I supposed, Julie and I looked almost identical to Joanna. How could I help but feel pretty? I couldn't deny that my reflection…that I was beautiful. Something at the back of my mind was trying to tell me that something important had changed but the effect of the pink pills weren't allowing any annoying difficult thoughts through. It must be a culmination of lots of little things to make me more perfect for Joanna that I was suddenly feeling all at once – the change of hair colour and style, the makeup, the subtle changes to my chin, the removal of that strange confusing flap of skin that had made me feel so insecure.

"Well, Julie?"

Julie was staring at my reflection in wonder. "She looks amazing! Beautiful!"

"I knew you'd come to agree with me."

Julie blushed, "Yes Mistress Joanna."

Joanna smiled at her and looked toward the bed. "There's a present there for you, Julie."

Julie beamed and turned to open it. Mistress Joanna squeezed me tight as I stood there still staring at my reflection, caught between wonder at how beautiful I looked and how much like Joanna as well as the odd worrying feeling that something wasn't right.

Joanna's hand slipped further round my waist and she moved behind me, both hands on my hips and her breasts brushing against my back as she looked over my shoulder, watching me stare at my reflection. She kissed my shoulder, then my neck, her hands slowly moving up my body to touch the sides of my breasts. I moaned softly as she did so, still looking at my reflection, seeing my breasts moving up and down and my nipples hardening, getting more turned on as it felt so much like looking at Joanna or Julie.

Joanna's hands moved onto my breasts, cupping them and caressing my hard nipples. I could feel her own nipples against my back and the tickle of the hair between her legs brushing against my bottom. She was whispering to me between kisses, telling me how pretty I looked, how perfect I was, how much like her I looked and how happy she was with me.

I was tingling between my legs and thought I could feel a slight swelling there. I reached my hand behind me, my fingers finding my way into the soft hair between Joanna's legs and my middle finger slipping just inside her, touching the little bump there in the same place I felt the tingling between my own legs.

"What's this?" I heard Julie ask in surprise. Joanna didn't take her hands from my breasts but she turned her head to look at Julie. I could see her in the mirror, standing by the bed holding something in her hand.

"What does it look like?"

"A strap-on. But why? And why so small?"

"Oh, I thought it would make a nice replacement for the loss of your…toy. A very *close* replacement for it…"

I saw Julie's mouth pop open as she looked more close at it then looked over at me. "No way!"

I heard Joanna giggle and gasped as she tweaked one of my nipples. She turned to Joanna and I turned as well, missing her hands on my breasts but intrigued by what was making Joanna so excited.

"I got them to take a cast before they…you know."

Joanna looked speechless for a moment then stared at the object in her hand. "You mean it's…?" she nodded at me, looking between my legs.

Joanna nodded with a grin. Joanna giggled as she stared at the object again and back at me. Then she giggled again, this time it turned into a laugh. Suddenly she was laughing out loud. Joanna was laughing with her and despite not knowing what they were laughing at, it was too infectious and I found myself laughing a little too. Joanna was in gales of laughter now, clutching her sides and sitting down on the bed, tears running down her face as she looked at the thing in her hand and at me, laughing even harder every time she looked back down at it.

She calmed down a little then held the thing between her legs with it sticking outwards and started laughing again.

"I can't believe you did this!" she gasped between giggles. "It's brilliant!"

She finally managed to mostly stop laughing, the odd giggle still escaping her lips as she tried to straighten her face. Joanna led me to the bed as Julie stood up and began inspecting the straps connected to the thing. It was a small pinkish cylinder, oddly shaped. My eyes widened when I realised that it was a…a…no, it was gone. Joanna pulled me onto the bed with her and we began kissing, making me forget about Julie, even though I could still hear her intermittent giggles as she fumbled with her present.

Joanna and I were kneeling on the bed, facing each other and she grabbed my wrist, putting my hand on her breast as she did the same to me. We kissed some more, fondling each other like that. She grabbed my other wrist and pushed my hand between her legs. As we kissed and I started to touch her there, I moaned in pleasure as I felt her hand touching me the same way, like we were reflections of each other doing the same things.

Joanna broke the kiss and moved her hands off my body. "So perfect," she whispered as she gazed lovingly at me. I was thinking the exact same thing as I gazed lovingly back at her. She shuffled back so that she was sitting up against the pillows and beckoned me to her. She motioned for me to sit leaning back against her and I did so, adoring the feeling of her breasts against my back. I was half laying on the bed propped up against Joanna as she kissed the top of my head and began fondling my breasts again. I lay there, my hands at my side caressing her legs lying alongside me.

I shivered as Joanna's hand moved onto my smooth stomach and slowly, teasingly slid further down towards the short stubble. I didn't like how rough it felt but I knew it would grow back and wonder if Joanna would insist on it being dyed pink again. I forgot about that as I watched her fingers move closer and closer to my…my…whatever it was called. I gasped as her fingertip touched the lips and moaned and writhed against her as it gently slipped inside and made it feel like my entire universe was focussed right where her fingertip pressed against the swollen little bump inside me.

Julie stepped closer to the bed. I glanced up and she had attached her present to her, a complicated-looking system of straps holding the things sticking straight out from between her legs. I heard Joanna suppress a giggle behind me.

"What do you think Jenny?" Julie asked, turning her hips side to side and making the thing swing a little.

"It looks a bit silly," I replied, to laughter from both women.

"Recognise it?" she asked, moving closer to me. "It's yours."

I frowned. "Are you sure?" I didn't remember owning such a thing. It was making me feel a little odd looking at it though. Looking at Julie felt a little like looking at a reflection of myself anyway but there was something about the thing she was wearing that made it feel even more so this time, despite the fact that I couldn't even tell how it was attached, let alone remember ever owning or trying to fasten such a thing to me. I was both utterly certain that I had never owned this strap-on thing but simultaneously struck by how familiar it seemed and the certainty that it did in fact belong to me whether I remembered it or not.

Julie smiled at me, "Don't frown Jenny dear. I know you can't really remember it. It's not yours anyway. It's mine now. It belonged to me for quite a while before Mistress Joanna took it away from you. I'm sure you don't miss it but I think I'm going to have fun with it."

I smiled, still frowning a little in confusion and trying to remember something but she seemed happy so that was what was important. My worries were knocked back out of my head as Mistress Joanna began rubbing me between my legs again.

"There should be some lube in the box with it," Joanna said to Julie. Julie turned and plucked a small bottle from the box. She popped open the lid and began applying some clear goo from the bottle to the thing between her legs.

I gasped some more as Joanna's finger pressed harder against me. Not really hard, just firmly. Her feet hooked round my thighs and pulled them apart. Julie climbed onto the bed, still rubbing stuff onto the strap-on as Julie grabbed me round the waist and pulled me further back against her, leaving my legs wide open and exposed to Julie.

"I can't believe I'm getting to use this. On *you!*" giggled Julie as she smeared a last bad of goo on it and shuffled closer. I gasped as I realised that she was about to press the strap-on against me. Joanna was still rubbing me with one finger, holding my legs wide as Julie pressed the tip of it against me. I felt scared and eager at the same time.

"Don't worry, I'll be very gentle," said Julie kindly, her hands on my thighs, caressing me and pressing the tip of it against me between my legs. I gasped and mouthed, "no!" but no sound came out. I felt the tip of it press against me and the wonderful, terrible, overwhelming sensation of it starting to enter my body. I moaned loudly, closing my eyes and laying my head back against Joanna, unsure whether I wanted Julie to stop or press it further in.

She pressed it further in and I winced. I heard her gasp and pull back slightly. I opened my eyes and stared at her, my mouth open and speechless. She put a little more lube on the thing then pressed forward again, slowly and gently as I tried to relax to make it easier, knowing that it was more likely to hurt if I tensed or resisted.

It went further in and I let out a long shuddering moan, writhing helpless against Joanna, impaled by Julie. It felt like nothing I recalled ever feeling before. It felt so wrong to have something inside me like this but so right, as if it were filling a void in me. Julie stopped and I lay there panting, helpless and paralysed, looking into her eyes a she looked lovingly at me. She began to move it out and that felt just as amazing as it going in but this time making me panic a little that she was going to take it out of me when all I wanted was to feel her inside me while Joanna rubbed me. She pulled it almost all the way out and I couldn't stop myself straining to lift my hips, to prevent the tip of it leaving my body. She grinned and teased me with the tip of it before pushing it slowly and gently back in, making me moan and collapse back against Joanna.

Slowly and carefully she moved it in and out, not quite pressing it all the way in or taking it all the way out, making me writhe and moan and move my hips in time with what she was doing, gasping as Joanna's finger against my little bump intensified everything I was feeling and I felt the pressure rising in me. Joanna's hand was moving faster now and I was gasping and panting then suddenly crying out as a massive orgasm rushed through me.

I lay back against Joanna, drained and overcome with emotions and pleasure and sensation, wincing a little as Julie carefully pulled back out of me and Joanna hugged me tightly from behind. Tears came and I clasped her arms tight round me as I sobbed at the intensity of it all – the love I felt for these two women, desperately missing the feeling of Julie being inside me, the rush of new sensations I had been shown. Julie quickly removed the strap-on and hugged me tightly from in front, wiping my tears away and planting kisses on my face as Joanna kissed my neck and shoulders from behind.

Joanna wriggled out from behind me and I snuggled in her arm, drained and sleepy.

"Are you glad to have the bandages off Jenny?" she asked me.

"Yes Mistress Joanna," I whispered.

"My beautiful, perfect girl," she smiled at me, pressing one of her breasts to my mouth. I took her nipple into my mouth, sucking and licking it gently as I curled up against her, trying not to yawn. I felt her wriggle a little, lying back slightly and opening her legs. I opened one eye and saw Julie kneeling and leaning forward to begin kissing her between them.

"I'm so glad Julie talked me into making you one of us," she breathed.

"Mmmm…" I sighed into her beautiful breast.

"You're my girl now. You belong to me. Forever."

"Yes Mistress," I mumbled happily against her nipple. All confusion was gone now. My body was perfect because it looked like Joanna's. What more could any girl want than to be perfect and to be loved like this? I looked like her, I sounded like her and I had the privilege of being her maid and serving and obeying and pampering her with nothing to worry about except making her happy.

There was no point trying to remember what I had been like before or what my life had been before meeting these two. It didn't matter and it couldn't have been any better than this. Trying to think about any of that only caused confusion and made me feel uncomfortable.

I could hear her moans at what Julie was doing with her tongue as I kissed her nipple and drifted off to sleep with a smile on my face. I didn't have to worry about anything now, Mistress Joanna would always look after me. I got to wear beautiful clothes for her and please her in any way she wished. She had made me perfect for her and I loved her for it. I was the luckiest girl in the world.

The End.

I hope you enjoyed this story. If you did, please leave me a nice review as I love reading them and they encourage me to keep writing!

Satinmaid

Other books by Satinmaid

Satin Christmas: Ash/Ella
Specially written for Christmas 2015.
Orphaned Ash lives a miserable existence with his legal guardian - his hated stepmother. His equally horrible stepsisters hit on a new way to torment him - forcing him to wear their clothes and makeup. As they try harder and harder to humiliate him he finds himself pushed into femininity and servitude with no apparent escape. But Christmas is a time of miracles and he may just have an unexpected ally.

She's the Husband…He's the Wife
A full length Satinmaid novel.
For her whole life Jeanette felt like she should have been male but had suppressed those urges and hidden them from everyone. When she finally admits her feelings to her husband Rick and tells him that she wants to be the man in their relationship he is shocked and confused.
Desperate not to lose the love of his life and determined to make her happy, Rick finds himself giving up more and more of the masculine aspects within their relationship to please her. She takes over as his husband and he finds himself slipping unwittingly into the role of being her wife and as her masculinity increases, Jeanette pushes him further and further into femininity.
It starts with little things like Jeanette insisting that she is the only one who is allowed to wear boxer shorts or pyjamas but his 'husband' wants more and the more masculine she becomes the more feminine Rick finds himself becoming.
How far will he go to please his husband and how feminine is he willing to become to keep the woman of his dreams, now that she is a man?
Jeanette is now the husband and if Rick wants to stay with her, his only option is to become her wife!

Turned Into a Girl at Claregrove
Feminised at a girl's school! Suddenly-orphaned Steven ends up moving in with his older cousin Samantha, a live-in teacher at prestigious Claregrove School for Girls. The loneliness of being kept separate from the girls and being tutored privately leave him depressed and the head mistress allows him to join in with a few of the extra-curricular activities at the school. His contact with the girls

is strictly supervised and he is under firm instructions to follow any rules to the letter - including wearing the Claregrove-approved tennis kit, which includes a skirt. Surrounded by girls, he begins to forget what it was like to be a boy but the clock is ticking. If his hormones cause him to become too masculine, the head mistress' concerns for the reputation of the school might find him banned from the clubs again.

A momentous decision must be made, one that will change the course of his whole life...

This latest Satinmaid tale is a sweet coming-of-age story for those of us who wished we could have gone to school as a girl.

Terry's Girly Job
Satinmaid's first full-length novel!
Layabout Terry is wasting his life and annoying everyone who knows him, so he is given an ultimatum - get a job or get thrown out of home. His girlfriend arranges a job for him in the office at the clothes shop where she works. What she doesn't tell him is that the job title is 'Office Girl' and there is a very feminine dress code that he will be expected to comply with. His boss is determined to ensure that he is wearing the correct feminine lingerie, his girlfriend wants him in the shortest possible skirts and even his mother is convinced that he needs help to accept his girly fate.

This 90,000+ word novel follows Terry's struggle to resist wearing skirts, despite the fact that everyone and everything seem to be conspiring to push him further and further into femininity. Can he escape the dress code and become a boy again or will he be stuck as an office girl forever?

Satin Christmas: Emma's Christmas Girl
Specially written for Christmas 2014.
When John gets snowed in at the cottage of his best friend Emma, borrowing one of her jumpers to keep warm begins an unstoppable slide into femininity as their long-suppressed feelings for each other are revealed and they both discover the sensual joys of John's increasing girlishness at Emma's hands.

Hannah's Girly Boyfriend
Anthony becomes Anne! Shy Anthony had never kissed a girl before and he thought his chance had come when the beautiful Hannah invited him to a fancy dress party...as a schoolgirl. The poor boy had no idea what else she had in store for him though. Will his love for

Hannah be enough to help him withstand the humiliations she puts him through and his slide into femininity?

Paul Becomes Wendy's Wife
An administrative error sees Paul getting I.D. in the name of Paula. Lingerie and sexy nighties soon follow but when he tries to rectify the situation, it backfires in a big way and he makes it MUCH worse for himself. Now he's wearing skirts in public! Can he get back to being Wendy's husband or will he be stuck as her wife? Can their marriage survive him being both Paul and Paula?

Monica's Sissy Husband
Exasperated and at her wits end, Monica wonders why her useless husband can't be more like a woman...so she sets out to turn him into one; to make him her obedient, feminine maid. This is a tale of a wife's decision to dominate, humiliate and feminise her husband but also a story of love and redemption.

The Spanking
His girlfriend has trust issues when it comes to sex. He promises to do anything to gain her trust and make her feel better but didn't expect her to insist on him submitting to a spanking to prove he was willing to trust her and to make himself vulnerable to her. By the time she wants to tie him up and put him in sexy girly clothes, it's too late to back out without destroying her trust. How far will he let himself be feminised and forced to submit to prove his love for her? And how far will she want to take it?

How I Feminised My Boyfriend
An unexpected obsession with a sexy satin nightie ends up with a young man being forced to wear it for his boyfriend. From satin nighties to sexy lingerie and more - an erotic tale of forced feminisation...partly based on real events in the author's life. Satinmaid Publications are proud to present an exciting new author - 'Girlmaker'!

Satinmaid's Bumper Book of Feminisation Stories
A gorgeous collection of six Satinmaid books comprising 12 short stories and 3 novellas. This bumper omnibus collection contains:

   Dancing In My Girlfriend's Mini-Skirt

A young man reluctantly agrees to wear a skirt for his girlfriend, not realising how far she intends to feminise him.

Sheila's New Girly
Sheila is angered when her flatmate makes fun of the transgendered patients at the clinic where she works. She decides to teach him a lesson in exactly what they do at the clinic and how a man can be feminised against his will. Resist as he might, Sheila's flatmate is going to become her new girly!

Not Always a Bridesmaid
When his best friend Jackie decides to marry her lesbian lover, she reminds Sam of a drunken promise he'd once made...to be her bridesmaid if she ever got married! Sam's girlfriend Helen loves the idea and he is helpless to resist as the women in his life make him more and more feminine. How far will it all go and will he be allowed to escape his reluctant femininity once Jackie's wedding is over?

Sissies in Satin: Volume 1
Sissies, spanking, submission and lots and lots of satin. An erotic collection of short stories about men forced to be sissies and dressed in the sexiest of clothes.

Sissies in Satin: Volume 2
Sissies, spanking, submission and lots and lots of satin. Another sexy collection of short stories about men forced to be sissies and dressed in the sexiest of clothes.

His School Skirt
Four stories of boys forced to dress as schoolgirls! Against their will, these boys are tricked or forced into girl's school uniform: A dressing up game finds Alan tricked into more and more feminine clothes. A young boy is forced to become a schoolgirl permanently. John is tricked into wearing the school uniform of the girl he fancies...twice! Includes the stories 'Pink Ribbons', 'Surrogate Schoolgirl', 'My First School Skirt' and 'My Second School Skirt'.